INTRODUCTION

Hello, reader. Thank you very much for deciding to pick up this book, whether it's for browsing purposes, in a library or you've spent your hard earned money on it, I am very grateful that you've made this decision.

My name is Dr H. Johnstone. I am a parapsychologist, investigative writer and spiritual medium who has decades worth of experience in the supernatural, unexplained phenomena and otherworldly oddities. I have heard and studied many stories over my years in this line of work. Some compelling, some mind-blowing and some being utter shite. But after so many years of people telling me their tales willingly, and quite proudly, it's got me thinking about something rather intriguing.

I was plagued by this niggling question as if it was poking my brain at every silent moment I had. I couldn't sleep, I couldn't watch television or even listen to music without this entering my mind. These questions ate away at me until I finally addressed them. Those time swallowing questions were - What about the stories people aren't so willing to tell? What about the people who feel too afraid or who feel ashamed of their true stories of the paranormal? Are there people out there who have kept it a secret their whole life? Because they're afraid of ridicule or losing credibility? I wanted to find out and I wanted to hear them all. Not just to feed my own morbid curiosity, but to free these people of their mental shackles.

So, I decided to come up with a way to explore this thought process. It took a few days, but I finally came up with the perfect solution. - Just ask.

I wrote advertisements and sent them to magazines,

Newspapers, social media sites, forums, even paid for a radio

advertisement in order to reach those who kept their secrets

locked away. Some of you reading this now may have even

seen or heard one of my adverts before, my advertisement

read as follows: "Ever see something you couldn't explain?

Ever have an experience that could only be explained using

reasoning that's not of this world? Perhaps a supernatural

secret that you are too afraid to share because of how people

may react? Well, my name is Dr H. Johnstone,

Parapsychologist, investigative writer and medium. I'm here

to tell you something you may not have heard before. I

believe you and I want to hear your story. If you want to tell

it, contact me via email at HJ@HJinvestigations.com. I look

forward to hearing from you."

After 12 months I'd received hundreds of emails. A lot of prank emails, some very questionable erotica, a lot of abusive messages and some blatant Hollywood style fanfiction but in amongst the hostile haystack there were some needles that were so sharp that they truly stuck with me.

I contacted the senders of those stories and was able to have very heartfelt and genuine conversations with them. I even got the pleasure of visiting some of them personally. We decided it would be a great idea to compile these stories into a book for the world to read. Most names have been changed to protect the anonymity of those who told them at the request of the individual. These stories are the ones that truly hit me in a way that I can't explain, they burrowed under my skin and clawed their way to my brain and wouldn't let go of my every thought. These stories are the ones that left their

undesired mark on those who lived to tell them. It's okay if

you don't believe, but these stories will force you to question

everything you've ever thought you knew of this world. - HJ

Story I – The Oath

So, I saw this advertisement online requesting true

stories that folks have been unable to tell others due to

their inexplicable nature. I've wanted to get this story

off my chest and out into the world for over 2 decades,

but whenever I try, I always have to stop myself,

because I know no one would believe me. How could

they? Even the police didn't believe us. I never thought

I'd have the platform to tell my truth, so thank you

Doctor Johnstone. Here goes nothing.

It was a freezing cold Saturday night in January 1995. I was sleeping over my best friend, Jackson's, house as I did almost every weekend. His parent's usually went out for drinks on Saturdays but this time they were away for the whole night and wouldn't be home until Sunday lunchtime. We were 16 and so excited. We felt really grown up having this opportunity to be left alone overnight. Looking back on it now I realise that we had no idea what feeling 'grown up' truly felt like. I was athletically built with a shaved head and wore tight clothes to show off my tiny lean frame and Jackson was lanky, skinny and had short curly brown hair, with thick glasses framing his deep brown eyes and a slight hint of a patchy moustache coming in above his top lip.

We had this secret plan to invite over two other friends of ours to hang out and sleepover with us, Alfie and Xander, who we'd known for a long time. But Jackson's parents had no idea. We figured we would all be outside hanging out by the time they were home so they would never have known. We thought we were being masters of manipulation when Jackson's parents asked us what our plans were "films, snacks and some games" Jackson said with a grin as his dad raised an eyebrow and said "You sure that's all? You're not going to go snooping for any of my naughty magazines again are you, Jackson?"

I laughed and looked over at my friend, his face was as red as a strawberry. "Dad!" He squeaked whilst glancing at me. Jackson's Mum lightly slapped his dad's arm as they shared a laugh.

As soon as his parents were out of the door, we both leapt up out of our seats and pumped our fists into the air. We put on a 'Best of British Metal' cassette tape and turned it up real loud. Then I went to my bag and surprised Jackson with a bottle of whiskey that I had managed to get from my older sister's secret stash. He was so excited that his face was practically 90 percent toothy grin and prickly tash. We poured out the lemonade and whiskeys and waited for our friends, Alfie and Xander, to come over. "Ah, freedom!" we said to each other as we clinked our glasses and waited for the time we'd agreed for them to come to the house. Not much time had passed before we heard a knock at the door, and we raced to answer it.

When we opened the door, there was no one there. We were confused for a moment, all we heard was the howling winds tumbling over the ice dusted rooftops and all we could see was the thick sheet of snow on the ground. It went deafeningly quiet for a moment, but then out jumped Xander and Alfie, growling like beasts! Jackson jumped out of his skin, called them both assholes & then started chasing them both around his front garden, picking up clumps of snow and launching them at Xander and Alfie. I wasn't that scared though. It took more than that to frighten me.

Once we'd finished laughing & Jackson had caught them both, we all went indoors in the warm & went to the kitchen for some drinks & sweets. We gave them their glasses of lemonade and whiskey and they delighted in the taste as they sipped on them. Xander was a heavy guy with a mop of curly ginger and wore the same dragon hoodie virtually every day of the year no matter the season. Alfie was a shorter guy, he had long black hair that he wore in a ponytail with a similar moustache to Jackson's and very light blue eyes. We'd finished our drinks quickly and poured out some more immediately before walking from the kitchen into the living room.

I remember a moment where Xander and Jackson went upstairs to look at Jackson's figurines that he was painting and left Alfie and I together. We weren't the best of friends, but we were okay. Although we had a big falling out the year before when he spray painted a wall at school after hours and tried to get me in trouble for it. But I told the truth and my alibi checked out, so he got the full brunt of the punishment. Suspended from school and community service. We'd patched things up since then, but it was still awkward when we were alone.

It took a fair few moments silence before Alfie made a joke about our best friends being "total nerds" and we laughed about it. We talked about the latest instalment of the Hellsmoke comics series that we both loved to read before I made a joke about us being the real nerds in the group. I wanted to clear the air a little more but just before I could Jackson and Xander came back downstairs. They were talking about how awesome

Jackson's monster figurine was and Xander excitedly said "Your monster is huge! I love the colours!" and to the surprise of nobody Alfie added "Oh comparing cocks, were you? I wondered what was taking so long! But it must've taken ages to find yours, Xander!", he laughed to himself and I replied "you sound like you're speaking from experience there, Alfie." Which got a genuine chuckle from the other two and an obvious fake one from Alfie.

We all sat down in the living room with our candy and pop, talking for a good few hours about girls and school, comics, board games and movies, laughing and joking. We talked about ghosts a lot too because Alfie was obsessed with them, I never really believed in any of it, but we'd all talked about it so much that evening that when it got dark we put on a Horror movie; I don't remember what it was called, just that it wasn't that good, but I'll never forget the moment that Alfie asked us all a question. One that we never realised would be so pivotal in all four of our lives.

"Any of you guys ever done a Ouija Board before?" He asked with a devilish grin on his face. We all sat in silence & looked at each other. We all shook our heads no and Alfie confidently exclaimed "I understand. It's a big deal. To be honest with you, it's actually too scary for most people to even do. I've done tons of them, but not everyone can be as brave as me, unfortunately." as a blatant boast.

I, Xander and Jackson looked at each other and paused before laughed uncontrollably amongst ourselves. A combination of the alcohol, sugary sweets and Alfie's showing off made for great comedy it seemed.

Alfie then said something to us all that stopped the laughter dead. "Alright then, jokers. If it's so funny to you. How about we do a Ouija Board tonight?". The room fell eerily silent. All we could hear was the faint sounds of the wind, knocking the tree branches against the kitchen window and the music playing during the crappy movie's credits. Then Xander, Jackson and I all looked at each other again & continued laughing so loud that it sounded like someone had pissed off a group of donkeys.

Alfie scoffed at our laughter and in a mild tantrum he aggressively unzipped his backpack, got out his notepad & flicked through it erratically, scanning the pages with his beady blue eyes to find a certain page and when he had found it, he slammed the book down onto the living room floor. We all looked down in unison & saw it lying there. Alfie's homemade "Ouija Board". Well, it was more like 'Ouija Paper'. Regardless, it looked like it had been used a lot.

I looked up at Alfie as he sat on the floor with his arms folded, piercing blue eyes widened and his teeth clenched behind his tightly clamped lips. "Well?" He said, clearly mildly annoyed. I gave a nod, got off the sofa and sat cross legged on the living room floor next to the notepad. Xander & Jackson both followed, but Jackson was noticeably slower to do so.

Alfie then asked if there was a shot glass we could use, and Jackson was so quick to jump up and go look. Whilst he was searching, Alfie got out a lighter from his backpack, walked over to Jackson's parents' fireplace and took 3 candles. He didn't ask if it was okay to take them, but that was Alfie all over.

"Ah, I can't find any glasses small enough." Jackson said with a little too much disappointment, I knew him well enough to know that he was definitely not upset about not being able to find any. So, I went to help him look & found them almost immediately in a kitchen cupboard. Jackson laughed nervously & said he mustn't have been looking properly. I laughed with him, but it was a fake laugh. Just to make him feel better really as I could tell her was nervous. He began to walk back towards the living room doorway, but I put my hand on his chest to stop him and said "if you're not comfortable then tell them to stop. We don't have to do this." But in vintage Jackson style he patted my hand and said "I'm fine. Let's do it.". I smiled at him, knowing full well he didn't mean that, but we took the shot glass & went back to the living room anyway.

When we entered through the doorway, the curtains were fully drawn, the lights and TV were off, but the room was aglow with the flickering flames from the 3 candles Alfie had stolen from the fireplace. "Okay, I don't know if I like this, guys. I've got a weird feeling in my stomach about it all" Jackson said with a jitter in his voice, not through fear but with anxiety over telling someone he didn't like something. He always was the nervous one, always trying to please, but he hated that he was seen as such. "Oh? You're scared?" Alfie said with a side-eyed sarcastic sneer. "No!" Jackson barked. "I just don't know if my parents would like us doing this in their house actually" he continued with a frown. "What they don't know won't hurt 'em, Jax" Xander said in an encouraging, yet peer pressuring tone. With a slight hesitation and hands on his hips Jackson said "Okay then" and exhaled deeply as he sat down in the circle with me, Xander and Alfie. Although with four of us, I suppose it was more of a square than a circle.

We handed Alfie the glass, he scanned it with his eyes, smiled and nodded in approval. "This'll work" he said affirmatively. He then placed the glass in the middle of his tattered size A3 notepad & asked us all to put our pinkie fingers on the glass.

I went first with my little finger. As I said earlier, I was never really a believer of any of this stuff, so I naturally had no problem being first to do something as silly as put my pinkie on an upside-down glass on a bit of crumpled up paper with some scribbles on it. Next was Alfie & Xander who placed their fingers on top almost at the exact same time. Jackson was last and still quite clearly apprehensive, but he joined us with his little finger after Alfie widened his eyes at him as if to say "Hurry up!".

Once we all had our fingers on the glass Alfie took the sharpest intake of breath I'd ever heard, it was so loud that it spooked Jackson who then took his finger off the glass and covered his mouth as he gasped. Alfie snapped at him "Don't do that, you idiot! Don't ever take your finger off the glass unless we've said goodbye!"

Jackson was so taken aback that he put his finger back on the glass without hesitation and in his trademark sarcastic sass said "Yes, your Majesty" which cracked me up, not so much Alfie or Xander, but I tended to get Jackson's humour a little more than those two. After we were done being fools, Alfie asked if we were all ready and we all nodded with smiles.

Alfie closed his eyes for around 30 seconds & began mumbling something to himself, I thought it was just for show as it sounded like gibberish, but it could have been some sort of a prayer or something, I'm still not quite sure what it was, but before I could ask him, the glass moved.

"Hello" it said. Jackson froze with a thousand yard stare and said "Was that you, Xander!? Did you move that?" with a slight wobble in his throat. "No! I thought it was you!" Xander replied. "It really wasn't dude." Jackson responded with a gormless stare.

Then Alfie smirked and began asking many general 'Ghosty' questions like "How did you die?" & "how old are you?" - NO & NO were the answers to those, which made me dubious to say the least. But it was when he asked its name that things got strange.

"What is your name?" Alfie asked with an elegant royal accent. The glass moved very clunky & slow to the letters & it spelled out "Ethan". All 3 of my friends looked at me with a puzzling & accusatory glare because that's actually my name.

"Stop messing around, Ethan!" Alfie said. "I'm really not.", I insisted with a chuckle at how ridiculous it was that he took it so seriously. "Right. So, it has the same name as you?" Xander said. But just as he had finished that sentence, the glass moved swiftly to 'NO'. We all looked down almost in sync. Alfie suggested that I should ask a question next and again, I didn't really buy into this stuff, so I jokingly asked "are you a virgin?" but it remained on NO, which as 16 year old boys made us all giggle hysterically, even Alfie. But then Alfie said to ask a real question, "Okay, so what's your real name?" I said, still half laughing & it spells out 'Ethan' again. I let

out a tiny bemused chuckle & the glass very quickly and

forcefully moved to 'NO' again. So quickly, that it even

startled me.

We weren't laughing anymore. We were all very still

and quiet. For the first time I felt an icy conga line of

chills going up my spine. "Who are you?" I asked in a

much more attentive manner now.

It spelled out 'Y' 'O' 'U'. I wasn't sure if this was a prank

being played on me by Alfie and the boys, or if this was

just a moment of collective hysteria or if this was totally

& utterly real. Let me tell you, the fact I was even

considering this being real, made me very, very

uncomfortable.

Jackson asked Alfie if we could stop now & the glass shot back to 'NO' again. Alfie appeared to be a little unnerved as he said "Yeah, I think that would be best." Alfie said he needed to say some religious phrases to end the connection & just as he began, the glass began to circle the paper in a clockwise motion. Round and round. Faster and faster. We all asked each other to stop but we all insisted we weren't the one doing it and then finally Alfie decided to press on with the religious phrases, the glass went anticlockwise one time and, to this day I shudder when I think of this moment, the glass flew across the room, smashing against the wall.

We all screamed at the top of our lungs and Jackson was visibly distressed about the whole ordeal but was also understandably concerned about the pile of broken glass on his parents' carpet. He got up, swiftly walked over to the glass and said "We need to clean this up now!", but just as he finished his sentence, there were 3 very loud knocks on the front door that scared us all. It got Jackson so much that he fell on his ass in fear which made us all laugh.

After a moment I got up and said something like "probably just a neighbour who heard us scream. Be cool, guys." But then I answered the door and, just like before, there was no one there. This time though, Xander and Alfie were indoors with us. I said "Hello?"

but there was no answer, I was just met with the icy lick of the frozen breeze cutting through the darkness. I closed the door and walked back into the living room when the knocks on the door happened again, louder this time. It made the hairs on the back of my neck stand to attention instantly, but I marched straight back, unafraid, and answered. But it was the same again. No one there. I turned to Alfie and asked him straight if this was a prank or if he had invited someone else along without our knowledge, but he insisted that he hadn't and that this was no prank. He even told me he was scared which, for him, was a big deal and so I believed him. Because I was scared too.

So, we turned the lights on and blew out the candles. Turned on the TV to see if something funny was on to lighten the mood. But there was a strange humming noise coming from the TV. As I got closer to it, the humming got more intense. Then it became a loud ear-splitting ring like a fire alarm. It was so loud that made us all shout out & cover our ears.

Next thing we knew, the sound vanished, and the TV turned off. It wouldn't switch back on either. This caused Jackson to get even more mad, complaining about the broken glass on the floor and now his Dad's TV was broken and at that point he glances down and asks "And are those my Mum's candles!?".

Jackson asked Alfie to fix it, but Alfie said he doesn't know how. Jackson looked at him and bluntly said "You're joking right?" Alfie looked at Jackson with a lowered brow as Jackson continued "You suggested we do this. You stole mum's candles, smashed one of my dad's shot glasses and read about this stuff almost every day and night and you're telling me you don't know how to sort this now?" Jackson laughed to himself out of frustration, but Alfie wasn't laughing. Alfie said "I've never experienced this before, mate. The less attention we give it, the less power it has". Jackson stared at him blankly as I snickered at the exchange.

Tensions rising aside, this was all certainly weird, but nothing compared to what came after. The smile melted from my face, and we all looked up in horror as we heard footsteps from upstairs. Quickly going from one end to the other in the room above the living room, which was Jackson's Parents' bedroom. It sounded like an animal or small child running around.

It was definitely above us, so I suggested that maybe their window was left open, and an animal came inside seeking warmth but then Xander sarcastically said "Left their window open and an animal got in. That makes sense. It's the middle of winter, Ethan. It's snowing for God's sake! Not only is it freezing but most animals are hibernating too.". I shrugged and asked if he had any other ideas, but he just shook his head. Alfie was constantly staring at the ceiling and whispering to himself, I asked what he was saying, he replied "Protection incantation. I learned it from a book." I squinted and said "A spell book?" To which Alfie dropped his shoulders and sighed "Yes, Ethan. A spell book." I gave a side smile and asked if he had a cauldron or magic wand in his bag that might help. But then Alfie snapped that this was no joke. I went to respond when he heard a loud crash upstairs, and the room was under an instantaneous deathly hush.

We all whispered to be quiet and to listen. I was still trying to be convinced it was all a big coincidence or some kind of prank. I could see why it was so worrying and certainly was aware of some kind of threat but just couldn't admit to myself this was real. It went against everything I was brought up to believe. So, I stood as stoic as possible, until we heard Jackson's Mother's voice call to him. It asked him to come upstairs to her room in a shaken and pained voice. Needless to say, my legs turned to bloody jelly. I knew in that moment it was something else, because I knew Jackson's Mother wasn't in the house. She'd left with his dad around 6 hours earlier.

We all looked at Jackson, whose face had drained of all colour. He was obviously terrified. Then the voice called to him again. "Jackson, Honey, please. I need you to help me. I'm hurt!" it pleaded. (I'm getting shivers all over my body just writing this down) Jackson was shaking his head. The sound of his mother crying echoed from the 2nd floor. Jackson looked tearful,

sighed and said "We've got to go check it out, guys!" But

I whispered a sharp & high pitched "Dude. No!" and he

looked at me & hurriedly said "But what if it really is my

Mum & she needs help!?". I looked Jackson dead in his

eyes, tilted my head & said "Jax, we saw her leave with

your dad hours ago! With our own two eyes! How could

it be!?", I quickly turned to Alfie & Xander for support

on trying to talk some sense into Jackson but Xander,

who was generally quite a quiet guy, agreed to go with

him to check it out.

I remember telling them repeatedly that it was a stupid

idea to go but, despite my pleas, they did it anyway. The

two started walking up the stairs, Jackson first, Xander

trailing a step behind him, Alfie & I waiting on the bottom step watching them ascend the staircase & listening for any other peculiar sounds. Jackson called out for his Mum but there was no answer. He called again a bit louder, with a distinctively worried intonation, but there was once again no response. Jackson looked back at us with heavy concern on his face and quickly scurried up the rest of the stairs with Xander following after. We didn't see what was going on but heard the slow footsteps when they'd reached his Parents' room. Xander called down to us to say it was empty and we then heard him pleading with Jackson to go back downstairs with him. "Come on, mate. Let's go. There's no one here and this is giving me the spooks." Xander said to him. But Alfie and I had a heart-stopping shock when we then heard a door slam shut from upstairs and there was nothing but silence for about 5 seconds. The silence was sliced in half by the muffled screams of Xander & Jackson.

Alfie & I ran upstairs to find the bedroom door shut & rattling. I grabbed the handle, but it was white hot to the touch! I shouted out in pain, quickly pulled my hand away and told Alfie it had burned me, he looked worried, but he grabbed the door handle anyway and was able to twist it open with ease. Xander & Jackson ran out of the room and downstairs in a flash. Alfie hurried after them immediately. I followed too, but I was so very curious about the door handle burning my hand that I was fixated on it for a few seconds before going down the stairs. I watched as the darkness filled my peripheral vision and I stepped down the stairs one by one. My fixation then transferred to my hand because I had no visible marks, abrasions or anything, but I could still feel the prickling pain of burned skin on the palm of my left hand.

As I descended the staircase, back into the living room, I saw Jackson & Xander hugging tight & sobbing uncontrollably. I asked what happened to them, but Alfie just looked at me & said that he'd tried asking them, but they wouldn't answer him. I stood there watching them tremble together and catch their breath. Alfie and I had no idea what had happened, but we were terrified of what it could have been.

After a few moments, the guys loosened their grip on each other's backs and looked at us through tear drowned eyes. Xander said "we saw something.", "saw what!?" Alfie asked with a shaky tone. Jackson began to cry again and Xander said that it wasn't easy to explain. "Well, try!" Alfie said with a harsh shout, I asked him to calm down, but he told me to shut up & insisted again that they tell us what they saw. So, I stepped closer to him & told him to calm down again. His face contorted and he pushed me backwards and said "You're suddenly against people talking now? That's rich coming from you.", I foolishly responded by pushing him back which caused him to fall down on his backside. He looked furious but shoving him had hurt my hand some more &

when I showed my discomfort, Alfie immediately apologised & asked if I was okay. I apologised too and I explained what had happened to my hand, that it was like grabbing hold of a preheated grill from an oven and that it burned really bad, but there was no mark there.

Alfie's eyes got wider and wider the more I spoke.

"That's a Phantom Burn" he said staring at me. I asked what that meant & he said that it wasn't good. It meant I was "marked". It all seemed so ridiculous to me still, even though I knew now that it was real. I guess I just wasn't ready to believe it. Then Jackson walked over to me & checked my hand, he said he could see the burn mark. Xander could too, but neither me nor Alfie could see anything.

They said it looked like a symbol. Like a letter K with a

pointy hat on it. I thought they were being stupid for a

second & then I remembered how wrong I'd been about

all this up to now. I asked them to draw it on paper, so

we rushed to the utility room, scrabbling around to find

a pen and a scrap of paper.

They drew what looked to be a disconnected letter K

with an upside-down 'V' on its head. Alfie had never

seen anything like it before; but then again none of us

had. Alfie just knew a whole lot about this sort of thing,

he was always borrowing books about ghosts, ghouls

and hauntings from the library & telling us spooky

stories. But this had him stumped. All I knew for sure

was that it hurt a lot and was getting worse.

Jackson found some frozen peas in the freezer and gave them to me, but the cold seemed to hurt it even more.

I looked at Alfie as I gritted my teeth through the searing pain and said "You said it was a 'Phantom Burn'? What is that?" Alfie looked down at his feet and said "From what I've read, these usually happen during some kind of ritual. You get a pain that feels like a burn but there's no burn, blemish or bruise there. It.." he paused for a moment and closed his eyes, shuddered and continued "it never ends well".

I stood staring at my bare hand in horror but before I could ask any more questions, Xander frantically interjected and said "but that's all just stories, right? Not a real thing?" But Alfie just looked at Xander with his lips together, stretched them to the side of his face and shrugged his shoulders. "I really don't know. What did you see in the bedroom? Was any of that supposed to be real to you before tonight?". Xander slumped himself down in an armchair next to the fireplace & said "No. That was straight out of a nightmare, mate." Alfie gently asked what they saw and, after a brief pause, what Xander told us in the moments following that inquiry will never leave my brain until the day I die.

He leaned forward, putting his hood up and his elbows on his knees, covering his face with his hands, as he let out the deepest sigh and said with a rasp "It was empty.

The room. It was empty when we got in there. But it was so cold. Colder than any winter I've ever felt. So, I wanted to leave, I grabbed Jackson by the shoulder & as soon as I looked at the door it slammed shut and we screamed" as Xander got to this part of the story, Jackson began sobbing again & covered his face with his forearm. I immediately wrapped my arm around him for comfort whilst Xander continued "then we heard the sound of a woman screaming for help, but it sounded like it was miles away. It startled us, so when we turned to look where it came from, our world flipped upside down. The whole room, guys. The whole room was just gone. The bed was gone, the drawers, the walls, the windows, the floor. Everything. It was all just snow and ice" he paused for another moment to compose himself with a small cough "and blood. So much fucking blood, mate."

Alfie & I stood there stunned. I felt that conga line of shivers erupt into a Mexican wave of prickly icy chills all over my body. I became very aware of my heartbeat at this moment. Xander continued "Jackson tried hard to open the door, he banged on it, kicked it and yanked it, it just wouldn't budge. So, I came to help him & it still didn't budge. But the screaming was getting louder & louder. We heard something wading through the blood sodden snow like it was nothing." He began biting his fingernails and shaking his leg up and down as he finished that sentence.

Alfie looked petrified at this point, I can't say I looked

any better to be honest but Alfie was able to ask "what

did it look like?"

Xander responded "It was almost camouflaged in the

snow. We didn't see much of it. All we could see was its

eyes & its breath turning to steam in the air. I thought

we were going to die."

"Me too" Jackson added with a wobble.

"But then the door opened, and we got out!" Xander

said.

Alfie sharply turned to me & asked if I had seen

anything in the room after the door opened but I

hadn't. It just looked like Jackson's parents' room to me.

When I said that, Jackson & Xander looked defeated and

puzzled. Jackson asked me if I believed them, and I emphatically said "of course I do" because what choice did I have at that stage?

We sat in silence for a few moments, when all of a sudden Alfie snapped his fingers and went into his rucksack. Fishing for something like his life depended on it. He found a small paperback book with the title "Demons A-Z" written on it. He opened the book and looked up at us all, I suspect expecting judgement, but he got nothing but intense focus from us all, so he continued to flip through it. He muttered to himself as he quickly scanned the pages until he stopped on a page, stood up and loudly exclaimed "this is it!" to himself.

"This is what?" Xander asked. Alfie looked up at him and then straight at me and said "you mocked the board.". I frowned in confusion and Alfie continued "you never believed any of it did you?" I replied "No. but obviously I do now." But he quickly added that it was too late. I started getting angry and said "Are you saying this was my fault? Because it wasn't my idea to do any of this. It was yours!". Alfie snapped back that actually we had all agreed and that he seemed to recall me being the first one to sit down when we started. I stood up and got in his face, I was overcome with rage, he put his hands up to my chest and told me to calm down, but I swore at him and slapped his hands away. Jackson and Xander were telling us both to cool it down and then before we know it, we were all bickering amongst ourselves.

We were arguing about everything. The broken glass,

the graffiti, the Ouija board, everything. But the spat

was cut short by a loud growl emanating from upstairs.

snapped us right out of the rage, we were convinced

this thing was messing with our emotions so we

apologised and bumped fists. "This is what it thrives off

of. This is what it wants. It needs the fear. It needs the

anger." Alfie exclaimed to us. We all nodded, and I

asked what he had read in the book. He said "Sanguis

Redemptor. Latin for Blood Redeemer. You made a

mockery of its existence and, going by the legend, you

have a payment to make.". I was not about to accept

being indebted to a bloody ghost, so I said "Well,

bollocks to that. It's not getting shit from me" to which the guys laughed and nodded.

Time had rolled on far beyond our comprehension and eventually became totally lost to us once we noticed the clocks had all stopped working. By now my hand was hurting really bad. I thought I should call an ambulance, but when we picked up the phone there was no dial tone, only static. I put the phone down and tried not to show panic, I just smiled and said "Fine. Let's play it like that." So, then I had the thought to ask the neighbours for help, so I quickly got my coat and shoes on and went to go out of the front door but, to our collective horror, the door had gone. There was just a brick wall in its place. Jackson saw this & crumbled into a heap on the ground saying "I don't want to die" to himself over and over. I was confused so I put my hand on the wall, just to be sure it was really there. It really was just a cold, red brick wall, cement and all. The door had truly vanished.

Xander said "let's climb out the window!" and aggressively drew the curtains back in the living room, once again revealing nothing but the same red brick wall. The windows had gone too. At this point we heard a loud scraping noise coming from the room above us again. It sounded like something very heavy being dragged along the wooden floorboards and then it stopped suddenly. It was then that I was overcome with a sense of duty to get my friends out of this mess no matter what, so I quickly formulated a plot to get us

outside. I told them all to stay together in the living

room whilst I searched downstairs for an escape. But, to

my utter distress, every door & window downstairs had

vanished. It was like we were trapped in a large brick

box.

I began to panic so I ran into the kitchen and noticed

that the doorway to the garage was still there. I ran into

the garage to use the garage door but that had vanished

too. I felt defeated and just let the stress of if it all hit

me. I felt the tears filling my eyes for a moment when I

rested my head on the red bricks where the garage door

should have been. Just then, I heard my name being

whispered from the other side of the garage. It sounded

like Jackson, so I turned and looked at the back of the room. He said "come here, I need to tell you something." so I walked forward slowly and asked "Jax. What are you doing? Have you found something?" I could barely see, it was so dark in there and I had gone into a dark corner where I could just about make out Jackson's outline. Just as I got to the corner, the outline disappeared, and the whispers turned silent. I immediately felt a deep sickness churn in my stomach and my hand burned like Hell. I suddenly felt freezing cold and the sensation of heavy breathing on my neck as the words "Found you" cut the silence. I slapped the back of my neck and spun around, causing myself to fall into the back wall. I was shaken but I quickly collected myself for my friends' sake and went back to the living room where they were all stood waiting. I told them what had happened and that we were trapped down here, every door and every window had been taken and it left only one option. We needed to go upstairs.

Jackson and Xander were visibly unhappy about having to go back upstairs but I told them that we had to, or I feared we would be stuck here until we all died. "We are trapped and need to escape somehow. But the best thing we can do is stick together." I told them. Alfie grabbed his bag, putting it over one of his sharp skinny shoulders and readied himself, Xander agreed with me and stood with Alfie. Jackson was almost incoherent through his grief, but I grabbed him by the hand, looked him in his eyes & told him "I've got you". He wiped his

tears away, nodded and we all went upstairs together.

We tried to switch the lights on, but they wouldn't

work. We all looked at each other knowingly before

walking up the stairs once more. Every stair creaked as

if it had aged a hundred years in one night, consumed

us all as he approached the top of the stairway. We

arrived at the top and soon noticed the sudden drop in

temperature and that every door was gone. Jackson's

room, the bathroom, the office, all gone. Every room

had vanished just like downstairs and showed that same

red brick wall that had been in all the doorways and

windows in the house, however these ones upstairs had

begun to grow moss on them and were covered by a

layer of white frost. All but one room that is. Jackson's Parents' room. The door was still open from when Alfie got it open before.

"Guys. This is our only option." I whispered. Xander grabbed my shoulder firmly and said "Don't you think it's a little convenient that there's only one room unchanged and it just so happens to be this one?". He looked around in fear with the other two, but I replied "I do. But what choice do we have? There are only two options. Try to find an exit in there or wait out here to meet what's been doing all of this to us. Your choice." Xander looked at me as if he was about to cry. "It's okay, mate. We're all in this together." I said with a smile. Xander nodded and got ready to enter the bedroom.

I was hurt, scared and felt a little hopeless but I refused to feel defeated. I pushed the searing pain of my hand and all of my bad thoughts to the back of my mind so that I wouldn't hesitate to enter. I barged into the room and quickly snapped my eyes over every inch of the room looking for anything unusual. Then my tension and worries melted away as I felt an overwhelming sense of comfort. Because the bedroom window was still there! I rushed to the glass and realised that I could see the back garden covered in snow, the fruit trees, the football, our bikes, it was all there. I went to open the window, but it wasn't opening. It may have been locked, or it was being kept closed by something. I shouted that the window was there, but it wouldn't open and then all 3 of the guys rushed in to help. We tried with all of our collective might to open it, but it simply wouldn't budge. It was like it was closed with cement. So, we stopped trying.

"We are like lambs to the slaughter then. Fuck!" Jackson said as his breathing became rapid. "What's the next idea, Ethan?" Xander asked with deeply set fear clearly painted on his now pale face. Alfie was just staring at the ground and shaking his head. Seeing my friends look like they were all about to die, feeling immense levels of pain and worry made me feel immeasurably angry. So, without thinking, I screamed and balled up my left hand into a fist. I then threw my already agonisingly painful hand at the glass with all my strength, repeatedly punching it like a maniac until it shattered the window entirely. Large and small fragments of glass flew around us, some fell inside, and some fell outside, I could hear the faint twinkling sound as they hit the iced over patio below.

I looked at my friends with exuberant glee knowing that we finally had an escape opportunity and said "come on, it's open!" whilst gesturing to the window, but they all just stared at me with wide eyes and open mouths as Alfie, with a horrified expression, pointed and said "Mate, your hand!" I was confused, but I looked down at my hand and saw a deep wound with a thick shard of glass sticking out of my wrist. It was oozing dark red blood, but it was totally painless. I'm not sure if I was hopped up on adrenaline after smashing the glass or if I was in so much pain already that I just didn't feel it. Either way, I just wanted to get out of there.

So, I pulled the large shard out of my wrist, which did sting a little and caused more blood to flow out, it spurted into my face, so I grabbed it and squeezed to stop the bleeding whilst I used my foot to kick out the rest of the glass. I looked back at the guys who were finally smiling and told Jackson to hold my arm and told Xander to hold Jackson's arms as he climbed out of his Mum and Dad's window. He climbed up and sat on the ledge, dangling his legs down before holding Xander's arm and turning around and sliding over the ledge to lower himself closer to the ground. He took a few moments to get the courage to do it, but he eventually let go of Xander's hands and dropped to the floor below. He landed on his feet and fell backwards, but quickly stood up and shouted up to us "Come on!" from the back garden patio. Next was Xander's turn, and he climbed up by himself, was steadied by Alfie and me as we helped him to dangle down slowly, as he was the heaviest of us and we didn't want to drop him. He dangled and let go, landing in the cold, dark garden below. He landed on his feet in quite impressive fashion too. He and Jackson hugged tightly and called on us to hurry up.

Alfie & I remained in the room & I told him to go, but he insisted I should be the one to go because I was hurt, but my dad always taught me to never leave a man behind. So, I held his arm and jokingly told him either he climbed out now or I'd push him out and just hope that the other two guys would catch him. He gave me a half smile, patted my shoulder and stepped out of the window, using my good arm to steady himself, he opted to drop from the windowsill instead of dangling before dropping, so as he dropped to his feet he let out a groan as he hit & twisted his ankle, but he got up quickly and hopped to Xander and Jackson who helped him stand up properly.

Lastly it was my time to jump. As I climbed out to a

chorus of encouragement & sat on the window's ledge,

they all stood underneath to catch me, but I told them

to move as I didn't want to hurt them. They listened and

moved to the side. As I clung to the ledge & was about

to take that leap of faith, I felt something grab my

injured hand and I slipped, leaving me hanging off the

windowsill. Only I wasn't holding onto anything,

something was holding on to me.

I let out a scream & the boys below shouted up, telling

me to let go. "I can't!" I shouted back, "somethings got

my hand." I said with a pained yell. They stood back to

see if they could see anything. Just then, I saw someone

peer over the window ledge. Well, some 'thing' anyway.

It looked directly into my eyes, and I felt promptly sick, I could hear my own heartbeat getting louder and faster. I just wanted to cry. Seeing my fear, it smiled a curly smile, showing me its crooked, sharp, teeth that had blackened with rot. Its vile eyes were entirely milky white with bluish grey pupils & its skin appeared leathery with a brownish green hue and was cracking and peeling all over. It had irregular sprouts of white hair coming from its wrinkled head and pointed chin too. The smell was inexplicable. Rotten, putrid, rancid. Nothing comes close to how it truly smelled.

The boys were telling me to "just let go", as if they didn't see this mortifyingly menacing monster clutching my wounded hand. Just then, its eyes moved one after the other to focus on my bleeding wrist, it began to

squeeze and constrict its long, bony fingers around my

wrist, digging its jagged, broken talon like fingernails

into the injury and causing the blood to run down my

arm with such volume that I could feel it in my armpit,

running down towards my stomach. It's tongue slipped

out of its nightmarishly large mouth and behaved like a

snake slithering towards the blood. I felt the tongue

touch my wound, it was scratchy like sandpaper but

warm and wet too. It licked the lacerations, tasting my

blood as it made a strange sound. Its milky, soulless

eyes locked onto mine once more. Then, in one quick

motion, it snapped my wrist like a twig. Now this time I

really did cry.

The bone snap was so loud, I can still hear it in my head. My friends were screaming below me as I begged and pleaded this spectral bastard to let me go, but instead it slammed its elongated bony hand on top of my forearm and began twisting my hand around and around with its other decrepit hand. I can still feel every last millimetre of skin ripping and tearing from my wrist, I still hear the stomach churning popping sensations and snapping sound of my bones grinding, cartilage cracking and coming away and the tendons stretching before snapping off. My arm was almost completely crimson red with blood, and I felt like I was about to faint.

This next part gets a little fuzzy, but I do remember feeling the very last fibre of my skin tear away as I fell to the ground, leaving my hand in the grip of the ghastly thing as it smiled a sickly smile as I hurtled towards the ground. I know that my foot hit the floor, but I didn't put any weight on it. So, my leg just collapsed underneath me & my hip hit the ground with all my body weight sending a shock up my spine. Next my elbow and shoulder hit & I heard a pop in my ear before my head hit the concrete patio with an almighty thud. My vision went blurry & I heard a loud ringing in my ears. I looked up at the window to see the beast holding my hand up, almost as if using my own hand to wave at me. I heard Jackson shouting "Ethan! Ethan!" Xander crying "NO NO NO!" Then I heard Alfie pleading for help from anyone who could hear us. I heard that Xander jumped the fence to get help from next door and that's who called the ambulance.

You might think that the worst part was losing my hand, but in the moment, I don't remember it that way. I remember the worst part being the cold. I felt colder than I'd ever felt before, but then again laying on a patio in mid-January would normally be cold, but also the excessive blood loss would have added to the chill I imagine.

Jackson knelt down next to me cradling my head. He then took his jacket off and wrapped my bleeding stump in it. The last thing I remember is Jackson looking into my eyes and telling me "Hey, you. Buddy. Keep your eyes open. You will be okay. I promise you."

Then it all went dark.

I woke up some days later in a hospital bed surrounded by my family & doctors. Apparently, I was in and out of consciousness after hitting my head, but I remember when I was fully alert. My shoulder had been separated and I had fractures to my elbow and hip, I had nasty bruising on my back along with a nasty concussion. Apparently, they never did find my severed hand. The police questioned me, trying to figure out if Xander, Alfie or Jackson did this to me. But I obviously denied that, so it never went anywhere. They searched for an attacker but never got anywhere with that either, for obvious reasons. We were on the news though. "Drunk

Teen Sleepover Ends in Bloody Accident". Our local paper had fun making up the narrative for that one.

I gave statements to the police. We all did and they all matched. Two officers laughed at us, and one got angry and asked us if we "got off" on taking the piss out of him. The official verdict was that they believed we had done illegal drinking and taken drugs, then came up with a ridiculously unbelievable story to draw the attention away from the illegality of what we did that night. It was humiliating to be honest. I was always stared at and talked about in my town. No one believed us and we were just seen as fools. I was even told by my grandma that I "deserved" what I got for being so stupid.

But that all happened 26 years ago now. 1995. I moved

away in my early 20s and never really spoke much about

it after. Xander drifted away from us all afterwards, he

almost instantly became a stranger to us all. I haven't

talked to him in 25 years. Alfie stuck around for a very

short while, but he soon went to college, met someone

special, got married at 18 & moved on with his life.

Didn't hear from him again either. He and his wife have

4 children, a very successful business and live in a huge

stately home in Florida now so my Mum tells me.

Jackson, though. Jackson never made it out of '95. Not

truly. His parent's came home early to find their home

in tatters. Broken glass in the living room & their

bedroom window smashed. Apparently, his Mum was mad about her candles being used too, as if that was important at a time like that. But that was the least of their worries after they'd seen all the blood on the walls, their ceiling and in their garden. It was everywhere. His parent's separated in June of that year, officially divorced later too. Jackson went to counselling sessions, but no one believed his story about that night either. His parent's just blamed themselves for always fighting & never showing enough attention to him so they thought he'd cooked up the story for attention. No one believed any of us. They just shoved pills and counsellors at us and chalked it up to drunk drugged up kids being stupid, ending in a tragic accident. Despite there being only a fraction of alcohol in our systems and zero drugs whatsoever.

Eventually Jackson convinced himself that none of it happened and that he was just crazy. He thought we had all played this elaborate joke on him, even though this "joke" would have cost me my left hand, there was no talking him down from the ledge he'd climbed to.

He disappeared shortly after telling us all he didn't want to know us anymore. I still remember the distant stare in his eyes as he walked away and told me "Goodbye forever, Ethan", I laughed and thought he would calm down and call me later that evening like usual. But here we are 22 years later and I'm still waiting for that call. If it does ever come, I will answer it in half a heartbeat. I miss him.

Me though, I'm alright.

Literally, now that I only have my right hand, but that joke gets tired after the 3rd or 4th time you use it. Let alone the 6,000th.

I live a simple life. My parents were so mad at me and never let me forget it. It strained our relationship, but it did get better when I moved out. When I was 21 I moved to Brighton to attend university and study engineering. I finished with flying colours and started my own company making prosthetic limbs. 5 years after graduating, I got married to a wonderful woman who I'd met at uni and we had a beautiful baby boy a year later. He's 10 years old now. We named him Jack in honour of my dear friend who was lost in more ways than one.

I think the main thing I learned after that night, was not to take anything for granted. Be it friends, fun, life or the limbs I am blessed to have left. Also, I learned never to play around with things I don't understand. My ignorance has cost me more than anyone could ever truly comprehend in the grand scheme of it all. I won't let it cost me or anyone else I love ever again.

Jackson, I know your name has been changed in this story to protect your identity but if you ever read this, please know that I love you and I want to hear from you. I miss you more than you could ever truly know. I just want to know that you're okay. My doors always open to you, mate.

Thank you for this opportunity to finally tell my story, Doctor. I am forever grateful to you.

- 'Ethan'

Doctor's notes -

When I first received this in my email inbox, I believed it was fiction. Until I reached out and spoke with the gentleman and his lovely wife on a video call regarding

this tale. There was no hint of falsehood about them or

their experiences. The gentleman's wife explained that

he sometimes talks in his sleep and the names of the

friends who were present in the story often come out. I

could tell this made him feel deeply uneasy and he didn't

want to talk about it at length, so I didn't press him

much on it through fear of triggering something within

him.

When I'd finished reading and dissecting this story, it

struck me as odd that 'Alfie' would mutter things to

himself that the others couldn't make out. He claims

they were prayers but I'm not too certain, that's not to

say they weren't prayers or incantations of protection,

but I still wouldn't wager a bet on it as I'm unclear as to what it was. As for the entity itself I am more than certain that it was a demonic presence known as a Dibornok. A very rare, ancient spirit that thrives on dysfunction and chaos. It is summoned using blood magic. So rare, in fact, that I've only ever heard of it through elite level exorcists and mediums I've encountered through my career. I've never read about it anywhere only heard the tales told to me by those in the know. The trademark trickery tells us that a Dibornok encounter was also likely due to the fact that their abilities are said to be so strong that they can alter the perception of reality around their targets. They're also able to grow stronger with increased fear and anger, which explains the physical manifestation after just a single night, it was feeding from the fear of four individuals.

But the true tell-tale sign of this being the work of a Dibornok is absolutely in the blood oath. The hand got marked, the hand got burned and the hand got taken. Why did it take the hand? Why did it choose 'Ethan'? This is why I doubt 'Alfie's' quiet words with himself being prayers. Because a Dibornok is called upon, they do not just appear at random. They are summoned for a purpose and require a payment. A deal made in blood shall be paid in blood. It seems 'Alfie' also gained a lot of fortune after this encounter too, which is just a little too coincidental in my professional opinion. But that's just it.

My opinion. You're free to decide for yourself what you believe. – H.J.

Story II - Betty

Today is a strange day. I woke up to the sounds of my wife's alarm clock on her fitness tracker gizmo. Which I didn't mind since we were due a major snow storm later in the day and I had to get up to walk our dog, Frank, and pick up a newspaper anyway. I get up, have my usual fuel of coffee and two cigarettes and get the lead out for the dog. Frank always comes running as soon as he hears the coat cupboard open, he knows his lead is in there. He's right at my feet at 6am ready to go out. I wish I had his energy.

So, I get my hat, scarf and gloves on, then layer a jumper with my big coat. It's the coldest weather Shawinigan has seen in 50 years and for a 67 year old gentleman who has dealt with many bone breaks in his lifetime, these old bones aren't what they used to be. The cold always makes them worse too but that's what I get for living in Canada. Regardless, I went on out, said good morning to my neighbours and made my way to the local store to buy my newspaper.

We got there around 6:45am, I picked up a paper with storm warnings plastered all over it, they just love to make a fuss over a flurry, but just as I turned to walk away, I was hit by a furious gust of prickly ice cold wind.

The wind smelled so familiar, it tasted like a bad memory and sent me right back to 1988, solo trekking the Saint Severn Mountain range and the attack that changed my life forever. I had vivid flashbacks of the single most nightmarish thing that has ever happened to me. I was 34 when I got caught in that snow storm in the mountains. I knew I could ride it out just fine but was attacked by something and to this day no one but my Wife truly believes my account of what happened up there. But it's 100% the truth. They put it down to delirium, but I wasn't delirious. I know what I saw.

I quickly snapped back to reality and looked down at my boy, Frank. I could see that the little guy was shivering something fierce, I figured that a Sausage Dog's, or a

Dachshund for you canine enthusiasts, legs were so small that his belly must be freezing, so I picked him up, popped him in my jacket with his little head poking out and carried him home. We got back just as the snow had started to fall harder too, so it was pretty good timing.

I locked the door behind me as I always did, put Frank on the floor and we both walked into the kitchen. Placing my keys on the table as I dropped the paper next to them. But when I dropped the paper, lots of inserts came flying out, the bullshit scratch cards that always somehow have you winning the jackpot, one flier offering new windows, and another was a magazine.

The magazine had all these crazy stories in it about escaping hostage situations, people surviving gang attacks and even some ghost stories. Not my kind of magazine, but my wife loves them. However, there was something written on this magazine that caught my eye. "Got a story no one believes? Send them here! Page 48". I figured that after my recall earlier on that this must be some kind of a sign, so I flipped through the pages to page number 48 and found an advertisement asking folks to send their stories to someone named 'Doctor Johnstone'. It said she was some sort of doctor and that she may publish the story for a book she is writing. I hadn't faced this in a long time, but that's twice in the space of an hour that I've been confronted with the memories of that frozen night in '88. So now I've decided to tell my story.

My story begins with myself at age 34, I was tall with a muscular frame and still had a full head of hair too, it was long, dark and curly, combined with a short beard. I guess you could say I looked the part as I spent most of my time outside in the wilderness. Camping, trekking, climbing, fishing, hunting. I did it all. I was quite the survivalist. I loved it too, the smell of the air, the sounds of the animals, the element of danger and betting on yourself. It was a rush. I enjoyed trekking the most. Just being outside with nowhere particular in mind to go, but just traveling for tens of miles on foot for days, surviving. I loved it.

My friends would always tell me I was crazy, but I never let that deter me. I was fine being the crazy outdoors person.

One evening in January 1988 down at our local drinking hole, The Jumping Jack, I was with my group of friends having some drinks. Gerry, Lacey, Tina, Ron and I would go there multiple times a week to hang out. The bar wasn't the most elegant of places to say the least. It smelled of stale booze with a faint waft of piss every so often, your feet would stick to the floor with every step, only half the lightbulbs in the joint would work and most nights had at least one fight. But it was still our local bar, and we would go there every Friday and Saturday to see one another, drink and have some laughs. I have so many memories of The Jumping Jack, but one sticks out more than any others simply for what came after it. We played a game, wherein we would ask a question of someone, and they had to either answer truthfully or drink. I forget what it was called. But when I was asked by Tina what my goal is before I'm 35, I told them I wanted to finally climb and spend a few days in the Saint Severn Mountain range. We all were very inebriated but managed to clink our glasses and drink to my New Year's resolution.

So, I'd decided I was going to finally do it. I was going to climb, spend time in and conquer the Saint Severn Mountain range, something I've wanted to do since I was a little boy, despite its notoriety and the perilous journey it would undoubtedly be. But I decided that I

also wanted my friends to join me on the trip and make

some unforgettable memories together. I waited all

week to see them on Friday at the bar to ask them. I

was so excited. I'd drawn up a plan, made a list of the

items they needed to pack, mapped out where we

would camp and calculated how long it would take us all

to get to the summit. Finally, it had gotten to 8pm on

Friday evening. I got myself ready in my usual outfit of a

flannel shirt, body warmer and some denim jeans, got

my brown work boots on and headed out to The

Jumping Jack.

I'd gotten there a little early due to my excited haste, so

decided to buy the first round of beers and grab our

usual booth. I set out the map and plan on the unpolished sticky table and waited for my pals to join me. Tina was first, she saw me and smiled made her way up to the booth. She wrapped her arms around me as she gave me a big hug. "This week has been a rough one." She said as she sat down. She thanked me for the beer, took a hearty swig and then gave a small chuckle as she glanced down at my map and plans, "You and your adventures. Where are you off to now?" Before I got a chance to answer, in walked Ron and Lacey, they walked in holding hands which at the time was still so strange to us as they'd only just started dating after being best friends for 20 years. I remember Tina made a joke as they walked in about the two of us getting together and competing with them to see who could make Gerry the most uncomfortable, which cracked us up but also made me feel a bit awkward as I'd had a small crush on Tina for about 5 of the 20 years we'd been friends.

Ron and Lucy walked up to the booth both smiling ear to ear, which was always real nice to see. They were both miserable for a long time before they started dating. But they were always amazing together, even when we were just a group of teenagers, we'd all secretly hoped that they'd one day get together and then one day they finally did and from then on, they finally looked relaxed and truly happy. It was like they were teenagers all over again. "Well, howdy" Ron would say almost every time we saw him, it got to be quite a signature phrase of his and Lacey gave us a big grin and tensed her shoulders as she usually did. They both sat down and thanked me for the drinks. We got to talking about our week and how boring it was at work. Then when Gerry showed up a few moments later we all jokingly groaned as if we were all unhappy to see him, something we did sometimes to whoever was last to join the group. He laughed and flipped us all the bird as we clinked our glasses in a toast to another week of work over and done with. We began our usual swapping of war stories from the working week. But the attention quickly turned to the maps and plans I'd placed on the table. "What's all this then? New tablecloths for the bar? How fancy!" Gerry said. "Oh no. These are the evil plans Al has to take over Canada and give everyone free beer" Tina jokingly added whilst taking another swig of her beer, that incidentally was actually free for her since I paid for it. We were all laughing except for Ron who looked at the plans, then at me and said "no, no, Al. I know exactly what this is. I'm not doing it." Ron was always the most nervous of the group, but I was offended that he'd immediately dismissed my careful planning before he'd even heard me explain it.

"Guys" I said with an enthusiastic warble in my throat. "We are going on a journey!" I said loudly and with a big toothy smile painted on my face. Instead of hearing the excited cheers that I'd imagined hearing all week, I watched as they all looked at each other in confusion. Tina looked at me with a furrowed brow and responded with "Are we though?". I explained that I wanted us all

to climb Saint Severn Mountain and they all just laughed

at me as if I was kidding. I was a bit upset as I'd put a lot

of effort into this plan and had been excited for a whole

week waiting to unveil it to them. I sat back in the booth

and sighed as they swapped one liners about my

suggestion.

"What's the problem, guys?" I enquired. The laughing

died down a little and Ron was first to say that they

didn't have the same level of training or experience that

I did, and that Severn wasn't anywhere near safe

enough for inexperienced people to climb. Lacey added

that people had died up there and that she won't be

risking her life for a hobby she's not even in to and

apologised immediately after saying it to avoid hurting my feelings. I understand her words now, but at the time I was feeling rather irritated. Ron agreed with Lacey, as I knew he would because Lacey held all the power in that relationship. I hoped at least Tina and Gerry would come along so I asked them both "what about you guys?" Tina shook her head and said she was sorry, but she couldn't miss any more time from work, I knew she wasn't being truthful, but I didn't want to push her if she didn't want to come and Gerry was looking at me sympathetically, rubbed his patchy beard and asked "Al, are you serious? Why do you want to do something so dangerous? Why not a regular camping trip? We can roast marshmallows, do some fishing? Bring our guitars? That sounds like a great time to me."

But I wasn't prepared to budge. I didn't want to take part in such mundane trips before I'd completed my life's goal. I patted his bulky shoulder and said we could do that anytime, but that I wanted to do Severn. I guess you could say I was a bit of an 'adrenaline junkie'. I told them that it had been a dream of mine since I was a boy, Lacey quickly replied with "Exactly, Al. It is your dream, but it's not ours. I'm sorry, Doll, but I'm not prepared to die for a camping trip." I saw the collective nod in agreement from the gang. They all flat-out refused to go with me. I was so disappointed that I got up and packed up my plans quickly, but the table was so sticky that my map ripped in half as I was pulling it up, which made Tina laugh a little and give me an empathetic sigh when I looked at her. I was in no mood, so I picked up the other half of my map, zipped up my body warmer and wished them all a goodnight. They all asked me not to leave but I was so disheartened by how they'd reacted that I knew I would be terrible company all evening. I could be very emotional at times. As I walked past the trash can, I shoved my map and plans in there as hard as I could and walked home alone in the cold.

I got back to my lonely little 2 bedroom house that my grandfather had left me in his will and went straight for one of the bottles of whisky on the shelf. I poured myself a few glasses and drew up some new plans for a solo trek up the Saint Severn Mountain range. I drank and drank that night. I was writing coherent sentences at first, but that soon devolved into scrawling all sorts of gibberish all over pieces of paper. I can't remember too much from the night, it gets very hazy, but I do remember that at one point I'd stripped down to my birthday suit and danced to some 60s Soul. I'd definitely drank a lot more than I should have, because I passed out at the kitchen table, buck naked, with a pen in my hand and when I woke up, I felt like death. My mouth was so dry that my tongue felt like it had a crust. My head was aching like I'd just gone 10 rounds in a boxing ring and to top it all off, my carefully written drunken plans for a solo trip up Saint Severn Mountain were stuck to my face, with dried saliva being the binding agent. It was the worst hangover of my life. I quickly grabbed my bath robe, chugged a glass of water to get rid of the dryness and turned the kettle on for some caffeinated fuel.

Just as I'd lit my first cigarette of the day and the kettle had boiled, my doorbell rang. I put my smoke in my mouth and stumbled like a zombie over to the door, opened it up and saw Tina stood there, dressed all in denim, with her short dark hair and big earrings to match her big smile. Her deep hazel brown eyes lit up as she said "Morning soldiers!" as if there was someone else stood next to me. I turned to the right and the left and didn't see anyone, "Soldiers?" I asked, Tina darted those same dark brown eyes downward and as I looked down, I realised my robe was wide open. I quickly covered up and Tina just laughed and laughed. I was embarrassed but she told me it wasn't the first one she'd ever seen and not worry. I was still embarrassed but endured it as I made her a coffee and offered her a smoke. Just as I passed her coffee over to her, she started staring at my face and frowning. She got up and walked closer to me, still staring at my right cheek and said "you're not going up there alone, Al. That's suicide." I was puzzled as to how she could know I was planning that just from the look on my face. I asked how she knew and Tina, stone-faced, just told me that she knew me like the back of her hand, and it was "written all over my face". I wondered if I was that easy to read and then she laughed and said "no, literally, honey. You have it written backwards all over your cheek." She went in her handbag and got out a small makeup mirror to show me. I looked into it and discovered that where I'd slept on my plans, the ink wasn't dry and ended up printing backwards onto my face the words "St. Severn Solo Trek". I shoved my face under the sink and scrubbed it vigorously to get it off. Afterwards, I got back to my cigarette and my coffee, and the conversation briskly turned from laughing at my embarrassment and drunken escapades to a very stern and serious talk.

Tina told me she had no doubt that I could do the climb but that doesn't mean that I should. She knew that I'd wanted to do this climb since I was an ankle biter, but she ran over the risks and the stories of people vanishing up there, getting lost in the wooded areas, succumbing to frost bite and hypothermia, Bears,

Mountain Lions, Moose. It was all stuff I already knew

but it didn't scare me, it enticed me. I wanted it more

knowing how dangerous it was. I told her that she was

welcome to join me if she was so concerned for my

well-being, but she declined my invitation again. This

time she told me the true reason, stating that she didn't

"have a death wish" like I apparently did.

After she finally asked me the final "What if" and I

returned it with an unshaken answer. She realised she

couldn't change my mind. I told her I was leaving the

following day. Sunday and wouldn't be back for at least

a week. She looked like she was about ready to burst

with overflowing emotions and then, to my shock,

quickly leant forward and kissed my lips. I was stunned. I asked nervously "what was that for?", she grinned and replied with her usual sarcastic dramatics and said that she would always kick herself if I'd died on the Mountain and she never kissed me at least once. I suddenly saw her in an entirely different light, that small crush that I never acted on in fear of losing my best friend instantly bloomed into something else entirely and my stomach felt full of flutters. She grabbed her car keys from the counter, walked to my front door, turned around and said "Be safe, soldiers", saluted, gave small chuckle and left the house. I smiled to myself and deeply exhaled as I added a bit of whiskey to my coffee before I took a big gulp.

The rest of the day was spent gearing up and gathering supplies for my journey. There was around 20 miles of hiking before I even reached the start of the climb. Given the snow and time of year that it was I also knew it was going to be a 2 day hike to reach the foot of the mountain, then it would take around 2 days to reach the summit. I was excited. In my eager confidence I thought to myself "I will do this. I've conquered everything else.".

I was packing just 4 cans of beans, 4 medium sized canteens of water and a can of meat. I had a tent that I rolled up and put on top of my bag along with my blanket that held significant sentimental value, I had my ropes, my carabiners, I had my boots and my many layers of cold weather clothes. I made sure to take a knife and my small hunting bow with a few bolts too as I was hoping on hunting some rabbits and eating what I hunt to get the full survival experience. I was also aware of the Bears, Cougars and the Wolves that inhabit the space up there. But I was well versed in how to avoid them, my tiny bow wouldn't have even done any damage to a large Badger, let alone a Grizzly Bear. So, I used the rest of the time to make a new plan using a map of the area, but I was sober this time and by around 9pm I was ready and satisfied. I sat on my weathered blue armchair next to my open fireplace, barely able to contain my excitement but knew I needed to rest, so I took myself off to bed.

My alarm went off at 5am, and I got out of bed like I was a 7 year old on Christmas morning. I was so thrilled that I was practically buzzing. I had all my stuff by the front door ready to go. I got dressed, made a flask of coffee, put three packets of Goldmyre cigarettes in my pockets and went out to load up my car that was totally covered in snow and ice. As I was clearing the light snow from my windshield, and warming up the engine, I found a note under my wiper blades, the ink had bled and was blurred but still legible. The words simply said "Please don't die. X". I instantly felt warmer in the freezing weather after reading that as I knew it was from Tina. I quickly unzipped my coat feeling the frozen whip of the winter air, put the note in the breast pocket of my shirt and zipped my coat back up instantly.

I'd cleared my car of snow and ice and had all of my supplies and equipment in the back. Within minutes I was on my way.

It took around 4 hours to get there, through country roads and about an hour on the highway. But thankfully it was so early and cold that the roads were basically empty. I just put my music on and cranked it as loud as loud can be. I sang my heart out on every slow or slightly romantic song that came on, as I couldn't help but picture singing them to Tina. Despite not being the best singer. I remember wondering if this is what 'love' felt like in those moments, but then a new song would come on and I'd start rocking out to that one and think I was just jumping the gun and convinced myself not to get my hopes up with Tina.

Once I'd arrived at the location, I searched for a decent place to park. I'd be away for a number of days and didn't want my car being broken into, even if I was in the middle of nowhere. It had just gone 9:30am when I found the perfect parking spots, hidden amongst some brambles and beneath a large Fir tree. As I got out of my car, I took my jacket off, put on an extra layer of weatherproof clothes, put my coat back on and got my bags on my back. That was the moment it all hit me. The air was crisp, the smell of the pine trees was thick, and the ground was covered in ghostly white snow. I felt like I could cry. I was finally there. I was going to achieve a dream. But little did I know that my dream would soon contort into a nightmare.

The bursting sunlight bounced off the twinkling snowy surface on the ground whilst I gathered my thoughts and began my trek into the snowy forest. Once I'd gotten under the thick trees the ground wasn't nearly as white due to the tree tops blocking most of the snowfall. Which made it much easier to hike through. I noticed there was a bright rainbow striped tent close to the treeline with a burnt out campfire next to it. It made me feel less crazy to know there were other explorers out here, especially in this weather. But I didn't disturb them, I just silently wished them a happy trail and continued my journey into the woods.

I could hear the distant calls of a few wild birds and noticed the dead leaves and thick brownish grass that lay on the ground underneath the thick foliage, but mostly I noticed the deafening silence. I loved it. I loved being one with nature and the feeling of being so very isolated almost felt like a home away from home. I wasted no time in starting to hike on into the forest, I'd walked for around 10 or so miles when I noticed some animal tracks on the ground. I knew immediately they belonged to a very large Moose, which could lead to some serious danger if I carried on following it as they can be very aggressive, and I knew my tiny bow wouldn't do much to fend off a giant the likes of a Moose. So, I decided to turn north west of the tracks and head through the trees, which lead me to the start

of a very awkward and difficult uphill hike. But I

embraced that, I lived for the challenges most would

deem too dangerous. So, I began my ascent to the next

level of this adventure, a decision I would later regret

for the rest of my life.

I was 35 years old, but still quite an immature 35 year

old. I had no kids, no girlfriend, lived in a home gifted to

me by a deceased relative, sure I had a job at a local

tourist centre but outside of work I essentially lived my

life in the bushes or at the bar. I had no reason to weigh

up my decisions because my choices never really had

much impact on anyone else but myself. So, up the hill I

went. Around 75 feet. It was much, much colder up

there and the wind had picked up tremendously. I remember one rogue gust almost knocked me off the side at about 60 feet, which startled me, but I laughed it off as I always did when I was face to face with danger.

It was around 5pm when dusk began to show itself. The sky had turned a peachy orange and the clouds had gone a pale purple. I knew I had to find a place to set up camp soon or I would have been stuck in the dark and that would have been treacherous on its own without taking into account the many stories of lost, missing or dead adventurers on the Severn. I walked about another 2 miles, gathering every bit of dry grass and any sticks I could find. Then I noticed a pathway that had been made through the trees. There were broken branches and trodden plants everywhere and bushes were laid flat on the ground as if this were some sort of a manufactured short cut into the next section of the climb. I figured it was from the various teams of climbers who had come up here prior to myself. I thought to myself that they obviously knew the place front and back and were just making their own routes to the mountain. But I also knew that I needed to find a nice area to shield from the cold before the darkness fell in around 20 minutes, so I followed the shortcut into the treeline.

I went around half a mile in when I found a whole grove of Subalpine Fir trees that served as a wonderful windbreaker against the harsh gales that were hitting the highpoint of the hills something fierce. I'd gotten my tent up quickly just as the night fell and I was able to light a fire very easily with my lighter and the dead grass and sticks that I'd found earlier. Luckily, with all the broken branches all over the floor, I had a decent supply of wood available to top up the fire as the night went on too. I hadn't seen any rabbits on my way up here, so only had my canned goods to eat for the night. Which I didn't mind at all. I sat on my trusty blanket and ate my baked beans, sparked up a few smokes and wrote in my journal about the day that I'd had. I wrote about the moose tracks and the other campers, the beautiful scenery and the unexpected pathway I'd inadvertently stumbled upon. After I'd finished the entry in my diary, I took a moment to take in the darkness and the reality of my childhood dream being in front of me, then I

decided to turn in and grab some shut-eye for the

morning's long trek.

I was nestled in real tight in my sleeping bag with my

thick woollen blanket pulled up around my head like a

swaddled new-born. I'd managed to pull some fallen Fir

branches around the tent to act as an extra barrier from

the elements, whilst simultaneously semi camouflaging

my dark green tent. I was in a deep sleep and dreaming

vividly about Tina. I remember the dream so well. We

were walking hand in hand in our local park, the day

was warm and there were kids playing all around us.

The birds were singing, and the sky was a vibrant shade

of blue. But all of a sudden Tina's smile dropped and

turned to a look of shock. Her face became sunken and
pale as the sky began to turn ominously grey. The kids
all stopped playing immediately, their basketball
bouncing away from them, their skipping ropes just
dropped on the ground as they suddenly all began
staring at me. Then they all started screaming in unison,
it was horrific. I woke up in a panic with my blanket
completely over my head but could still hear the very
same screaming sounds coming from around 20 yards
from my tent.

Screaming. Only I knew this wasn't from a human, I
could tell this was a distressed animal. At first all I'd
heard was the scream, it was unlike anything I'd ever
heard in my life, but then I heard the snapping of

branches along with some multi-tonal grunting and growling. I then realised that there was a fight going on outside my tent. For the first time that I could remember, I felt genuine terror sweep through my body at the moment I heard the unmistakable defensive roar of an adult Grizzly Bear.

I knew I had to stay inside my tent and be very still. I began to slowly slide the blanket off of my sweating head so my eyes could see the entrance to my zipped up tent, I heard more shuffling of twigs and rocks, snapping branches and some harsh, throaty growls. Then suddenly there were a few painful whimpers appearing to get louder followed by a loud, heart wrenching thud drawing nearer to my tent. I was convinced they were going to land on my tent and crush me. I was shaking and my heart was beating out of my chest. I could barely control my breathing when I heard the sounds come no more than 3 or 4 yards from my tent, All I could do was pray they'd take it elsewhere. I was horrified when I heard another big thud on the floor that physically vibrated the ground I was sitting on. But instead of crushing me in my tent, it all fell eerily silent. I couldn't hear a thing except the creaking of branches as they swayed in the winter winds for about 30 seconds. But then something pierced the moonlit forest like nothing I'd ever even imagined before. A sound that began as a high pitched squeal and ended in a guttural rumbling roar. I had no idea what could make such a sound, but it sent pure, unadulterated terror through my body like a bolt of lightning. I finally heard the bear give one final grunt before it yelped like a dog who'd had its paw stepped on and then my ears were met by the sound of a very loud snap.

I was statue still. Frozen in temperature and in fear. I could hear the warbling deep breathing of a beast just outside my tent, it made some more noises that sounded like chirruping, as if it was still somehow willing the bear to continue their battle, but the bear was dead silent. After that I heard more snapping noises and the sounds of what I can only describe as a wet towel being dropped on a stone floor over and over. What followed was the sound like the crackling pop of a fork going into saucy spaghetti, only a lot louder. I had no idea what was happening, I just knew I had to stay put and stay

quiet.

After about 20 minutes, the beast's grunting had

stopped and all I could hear were the thunderously

heavy footsteps of this creature outside my tent getting

further away and the echoes of snapping branches

growing distant. But I didn't do anything except get out

my journal and write down what had just happened. I

referred to it as a 'bear fight', because that's all I could

think that it was. That was until I went outside.

I stayed in my tent until I could see the sunlight beaming

through the material on my miraculously unscathed

tent. I was relieved when the sun rise began, but that vanished very quickly when I emerged from my tent to find the snowy trail painted red and pools of deep crimson dotted around the site. I figured it must've been a fatal fight between the bears anyway, but then I walked around the corner of the trees to discover the mangled carcass of a Grizzly Bear. The thing was about 8 foot and around 700lbs, its stomach was torn open and it's innards were scattered all over the floor, it had huge chunks taken out of its neck and back, so deep that it had almost been decapitated. But the most disturbing part was the moment I had realised that it's head was twisted upside down and it's right front leg had been torn off and was nowhere to be found. I stumbled backwards in shock as I asked myself what could have done this much damage to an Apex predator like a 700lb Grizzly Bear. I didn't know what else to do besides spark up a smoke, get out my journal and document what I was seeing.

In the 80s, we didn't have cameras on everything like we do now, and I didn't bring any cameras with me, I just sketched and wrote down what I saw as I did with virtually everything. So, after drawing a quick sketch of what I'd seen, I gathered all of my things in a hurry and quickly set off back in the direction I entered. I decided to leave whatever territory I had stumbled into and continue with my mapped out journey. "No more short cuts" I said to myself as I got out into the open again, giving one more fleeting glance at the path I'd just left behind and shuddered before embarking on the rest of my trip.

I continued on my planned path for nearly 4 more miles, it was almost completely uphill, and I was completely exhausted from the lack of sleep from the previous night. I couldn't stop hearing the sounds of the bears final moments on repeat in my mind. Its whimpering, its painful groans, that's when I realised that the snapping sounds and wet towel sounds were the sounds of this animal being ripped apart. I wondered what on earth could have done it but figured that I would never truly know. It was the grisliest scene I'd ever witnessed, no pun intended.

By the time the sun had fully risen I'd managed to reach the top of the steep and snowy hill. I'd been walking for hours and was delighted to see that I could finally tread on flat ground with a straight shot to the mountain's edge. It looked like the perfect place to set up camp and catch up on some much needed rest. The sun was up, the snow was thick, and the air was crisp; all seemed perfect up there. I walked the distance to the bottom of the mountain and set up camp under a large pine tree. It wasn't hard to choose where to set up, not only was the tree large in size so it was the perfect windbreaker, but it smelled so fresh and inviting that I simply couldn't resist.

I set up my tent and gathered some sticks for the fire I'd

be starting in a couple of hours. Once I'd brought the

sticks back to the campsite my eyes wandered upwards,

and astonishment took over. My hands lost their clutch

on the twigs, and they all scattered all over the

frostbitten ground; The site of the legendary Saint

Severn Mountain took my breath away. I could hardly

believe that I was so close to something I'd only ever

seen in books and my frequent daydreams. I remember

feeling a great sense of not only pride but also of

gratitude. I'd made it. I had some scary moments over

the past two days, but at long last I had made it to the

start of my journey. I was so overcome with emotion

that the close call with the bears from the previous

night didn't even enter my line of thought for a good 20 minutes.

I was suddenly whipped by the frosty chill of the hillside winds. The air was much colder and almost painful up there, so I was forced back into real life quite aggressively. I decided that I had done enough setting up and wanted to rest before the night and days ahead. I wanted to sit down and bask in the unwavering beauty of this location, so I went to get my trusty blanket out of my backpack to use as a buffer between my buttocks and the frozen ground. I looked in my pack, but I didn't see my blanket. So, in a panic, I had gotten everything out of the backpack but still no sign of it. I then checked on the floor around the area, but it was nowhere to be seen. I realised then that I must have left it behind in my haste to leave the site of the blood soaked bear massacre that morning. I was devastated by this because that blanket had been with me for almost two decades and was almost like a travel companion. It went everywhere with me. Camping trips, fishing trips, vacations, trekking, absolutely everywhere for almost 20 years. So, losing it felt very much like losing a piece of myself. I even considered going back for it but knew it was a fool's errand risking my life for a blanket, regardless of the memories attached to it.

I sat and reminisced on all of the fun times I'd had and how many memories that blanket had been a part of. My mountain climbs, ski trips at Christmas with my family, camping and night fishing with my dad, I even lost my virginity under the thing. I smiled to myself thinking back to those times as the sun was coming down, disappearing behind the jagged edge of the mountain. I sat and lit my fire using my lighter, basic wood and dried grass as kindling. It heated the ground and melted the snow around it very quickly, so I sat smoking whilst watching the embers crackle and burn. Before I knew it, the night had truly fallen and just as I was smoking my 4th cigarette and stoking the flames of my campfire, I heard a squeak. A very familiar squeak. It was the squeak of a Mountain Rabbit.

I was excited to finally get the thrill of a hunt on this trip and experience the survival elements to the fullest. I dropped and stomped my cigarette out gently so as to

not startle the Rabbit, hearing the lit end sizzle gently

on the snow. I then quickly grabbed my bolts and my

small bow from the tent and peered around the edge of

the entrance. I saw the little guy hopping around and

sniffing for vegetation, just minding its own business.

Little did it know that it had become *my* business. So, I

pulled up my bow, loaded it up and cranked back on the

bowstring with a bolt and watched it move. Once I'd

lined up the sights and had a clear shot at the rabbit, I

was ready to fire. But just as I released and let it fly a

huge gust of ice cold wind hit me hard causing me to

shudder and botch the shot. I had missed the Rabbit,

shot the bolt next to the animal which was more than

enough to spook it, so it ran away. Being the arrogant

moron that I was in my youth, I decided to follow on

and continue hunting the fleeing rabbit, following its

tracks in the snow until I reached the trees where the

snow got thinner. But to my disappointment, suddenly

I'd discovered that there were no prints left to track at

all. It was like the bunny had just disappeared. I looked

around, crouched down, patted the ground to see if its

burrow was around there under the snow, but there

was nothing. It totally vanished.

The sun had all but completely gone down by now and

all that remained was the faint glow from my campfire

brushing up against the icy tree line. I had a feeling of

unease in my stomach and wanted to return to my

camp. I don't know if it was foresight or just the spooky

sight of a darkened solemn forest, but I instantly made my peace with having baked beans for dinner again and decided to return to camp. I was heading back when I heard the squeaks of the rabbit once more. I swiftly turned my head and saw it hop out from behind a nearby tree, so I picked up my bow, yanked back on the string and aimed at its head one last time. The rabbit stood still, giving me the perfect shot but then, within a second and to my utter disbelief, a massive furry hand slammed down on top of it, then slowly scrunched up its fingers into a fist and then, as it picked up its rodent prize, I saw in amongst the shadows that it was reaching up towards a mouth of long tusks and pointed teeth. I stood staring in horror whilst the rabbit was shoved into the blackened jaws of this animal. I watched on in a state of psychological paralysis as the blood and guts gushed out over the lop-sided tusks and jagged teeth of this monstrosity and the sound of crunching bones amplified around the small forested area.

I stood perplexed at what had just happened. Then out of the shadows stomped a creature that I had never seen in any wildlife books or on television and still haven't even to this day. It was around 15 foot tall and as wide as a monster truck. It had blueish grey skin that was layered with thick, matted white fur that had clearly been stained with various dried blood spatters, dirty waters and aged mud. It had 2 white eyes, a huge mouth with two twisted tusks either side of its bottom jaws and rows of pointed, serrated teeth in its massive mouth. I froze for a moment in disbelief of what I was seeing, I stared at this gargantuan beast that was staring right back at me. It began sniffing the air and grunting after each inhale whilst puffs of mist exited through its large dark nostrils on every exhale. Oddly though, despite its lingering death stare I didn't feel like it was truly watching me, however it appeared to have spotted me as I took a singular step backwards and my boot crunched against the fallen snow, it's ghostly white eyes widened, it opened its blood-stained mouth and emitted a sound that made my blood run cold. A high pitched scream that descended into a guttural growl, It was at that moment that I quickly realised this was the same creature that had attacked and decimated the Bear outside my tent the previous night, or at the very least it was the very same species. I didn't know what to

do but I knew that I was in some serious trouble.

I thought on my feet and figured I needed to act fast.

So, with my shaking arms I lifted my tiny small game

bow and fired a bolt into the monster's greyish blue

chest, but it just bounced off like I'd thrown a screwed

up piece of paper at a wall. Despite the lack of any

damage, the beast wasn't happy that I'd done that. It

grumbled and growled at me again, placing it's long

arms on the ground and lowering its head looking like it

was about to pounce. I lost all my senses in that

moment and just turned my back on the snarling

menace in order to make a run for it, which in hindsight

I know was a very stupid move. It caught me in around 7

seconds, grabbing my lower left leg as I was running and so I fell face first into the snow. The instant pressure around my shin bone was immense, like a mechanical vice being tightened around it. The firm grip on my leg and the sharp flakes of the settled snow on my face were nothing compared to what came next. Before I could even register my next thought, I was being lifted up, upside down by one leg and around 8 feet off the ground.

Time almost stood still for a moment, I felt the chill of the mountain on my face and the warmth of my clothing against my skin but that was all shattered in seconds as I was quickly and violently slammed back down into the frozen ground below and picked up again within an instant. I saw a big white flash in my eyes and could hear a loud ringing sound in my ears on the second slam as the beast continued with its ruthless onslaught. On the sixth slam though, it let me go. I was face down in the snow gathering my breath for a second, wondering if it had lost interest and left, but then its large palm swiped at my arm, the force of which turned my whole body 180 degrees, so I rolled over onto my back just as its ginormous, thick talon-like claws came striking down and tore through the four layers of clothes I had on but luckily avoided my skin underneath. I screamed and tried to get to my feet, but it knocked me right back down again with a slap on my chest. It didn't seem to like it when I screamed. I reached for my quiver of bolts but, to my horror, it was too far away. So, I rolled my body over onto my front

once more and crawled on my hands and knees in a

frantic scurry to retrieve the small bag of arrows as fast

as I could. I got close enough to grab one and despite

knowing it did very little damage to this thing, I knew

needed something, anything to protect myself against

this monster.

But the moment I turned to face my nightmarish

attacker I was met with the same immense pressure of

the animal on my shoulders, as it pinned me down to

the snowy floor and came face to face with me. That's

when I got a real feel for the size of this animal. It's head

was the width of the front of a small car and its hands

were 3 times the size of any bear paws I'd ever seen,

but I noticed that it had thumbs and they looked almost human, minus the size, thick white fur and blueish grey skin of course. As the light from my campfire bounced off its corpse coloured complexion and reflected off its milky eyes, It slowly opened its mouth inches from my face, I could see that it had rows of razor sharp teeth, not too dissimilar to a shark, and I could smell the putrid stench of death on its moist, hot breath. I was practically frozen in fear but somehow managed to wriggle my arm out of the sleeve of my coat and push it through the tears in my clothes. Armed with the singular bolt that I gripped firmly in my quivering hand, I stabbed the thing square in the centre of the flickering crystal that was its left eye. The beast instantly leapt up, releasing my shoulders as it wailed in pain. I took the opportunity to get up and run like Hell to my camp.

After around 10 seconds, I heard the thunderous

stomps of its mammoth sized feet begin to gallop

behind me as I neared the camp fire. I reached the site,

knowing it was about to get me once again at any

second. I quickly and without hesitation jammed my

hand into the roaring fire, picking up a log that was

ablaze and threw it at the beast in what I presumed

would be a feeble attempt at protection but, to my

absolute surprise, the beast recoiled from the flaming

piece of wood hurtling towards it and ran off into the

darkness. I was so hopped up on adrenaline that I didn't

even feel the pain at first, but I knew that I'd burned my

hand quite badly. I figured that was a small price to pay

for keeping my head though.

I kept the fire stoked and continuously grabbed

handfuls of snow to ease the burn on my hand that was

gradually getting more and more painful. I used my

small saucepan to boil some snow in a pot to turn it into

drinking water for my canteen, as it was boiling, I pulled

up the leg of my bottoms and saw the blood rising to

the surface underneath my skin as the deep, giant finger

shaped bruises began to form around my calf. I was in

rough shape.

I was unsure of whether or not it would be wise to

move as I had no idea where the beast had run off to.

But it seemed to really hate the fire, so I decided to stay

put by my heavily illuminated camp, smoke cigarette

after cigarette and gather my thoughts. I was under no illusion that I would attempt any more of the climb. I decided that my life was worth more than any mountain, but I was very much aware that I was around 17 miles away from my car, now mildly injured and alone on a mountain with a giant monster that just tried to kill me. It wasn't over. Not by a long shot.

The sun arose at around 5am, beaming through the branches of the forest that was around 50 feet from me. I immediately gathered my things and made sure I didn't leave anything behind this time. I strapped everything into place, got my bag on and readied myself for the descent. My leg hurt a lot. Especially now that my adrenaline had faded. I lifted my bottoms up to see that my lean leg had swollen up to the point that I couldn't see any muscle definition anymore and it was very painful to walk on. I knew this was going to be a rough time but since it was light now, I had the idea that this monster was gone and wouldn't bother me again, at least not until nightfall. So, I decided to limp over to the tree line and find a sturdy stick to support myself with. I tried many but they would snap or be too short, until I finally found one that was the perfect height and thickness to support my weight and frame. I breathed a sigh of relief and felt blessed to have some pressure taken off my throbbing calf and shin even at the expense of burning daylight. But I soon refocused and set about my journey downward.

It took me around 4 hours of painful walking, short breaks and the constant favouring of my left leg before I'd managed around 5 miles of the 17 or so I had to go. I was tired, hungry and exhausted. I had doubts at this point that I would ever make it home again, but I pushed them far away to the back of my mind, I remember at one point I slipped on an icy patch of the trail and put all my weight on my bad leg. I screamed so loud that birds flew out of the trees near me, and I heard my voice echo around the vastness of the cold and desolate mountainside. I hunched over and rested my head on my stick, holding back the tears that were fighting to fall from my eyes. But as I looked up, I was elated to see that same striped rainbow tent that I'd seen at the beginning of my journey.

I felt supremely relieved. I felt like I finally could get

some help. So, I quickly hobbled over the fallen

branches and snowy mounds on the ground to make it

to their tent. Ignoring the sharp pains in my leg,

shouting out greetings and asking for assistance. I

reached the tent and finally had some hope, but that

hope was quickly obliterated upon seeing the front of

the tent ripped open, the snow around it stained a deep

red and what appeared to be blood, flesh and bits of

bone scattered and spattered all over the inside of the

large rainbow coloured tent. I'm not sure if it was the

smell, the sight, the exhaustion or a mixture of all three

but I instantly turned and violently vomited on the

ground after discovering the repulsive and revolting sight.

I was quivering and felt a strong feeling of fluttering in my gut. I felt my chest tighten and I couldn't catch my breath, I was shaking and not from the cold, I was panicking and knew I needed to get it under control. I paused, took some deep breaths and held them in before exhaling deeply, I took a large gulp of my boiled snow water, collected my composure and after a few moment, I turned back to face the gruesome scene inside the tent.

I was close to tears seeing the brutality before me, when I noticed that their bags were still in the tent, entirely untouched. I couldn't believe my mind was going there, but it was, because I was faced with a rotten moral dilemma. I was in desperate need and was torn between whether to search these backpacks for food or first aid or respecting the dead and leaving their belongings alone. I knew the latter was the more respectable thing to do, but this was a matter of life or death, and I did what I had to do. In the moment I convinced myself that I was prepared to live with the guilt of robbing the deceased, so I searched their bags and found their clothes and hats which I had no need for. However, in the side compartments I found bandages and a small multi tool. In the other bag there was bread, tins of tuna and a half drank bottle of vodka. I took a few swigs of the vodka almost on instinct, then proceeded to grab the food, throwing it into my own bags. I took the bandages and multi tool also because I had a feeling they may come in handy, and boy was I right about that.

Just as I was zipping up the bag a photo of a man, a woman and a small child fell out and landed in one of the pools of blood face up. I quickly fished it out and looked at it. The words written on the back of the photo are still etched in my brain. They read "Mummy, Daddy & Maggie (age 3) on our Wedding Day - 1987". That hit my like a bullet. I was sat with the remains of this little girl's parents. I felt so awful for taking their things, but in the moment, I was realistic in recognising that, as awful as it sounds, I needed it more than they did. I thanked them, what was left of them anyway and despite not being that religious, I said a prayer for them. I promised them that when I found my way back, I would send people to find them so that their little girl would know what happened to them, this was an empty promise because I still was unsure if I was even going to make it back down myself. But I took the photo in hopes that I could return it to little Maggie.

I journeyed on, step by painful step, down the mountain range. After another 6 hours and probably less than 5 miles it was beginning to get dark again. Luckily for me I was near some large trees when the light began to fade, so I quickly searched for fire wood, but I was simply in no condition to go back and forth trekking into the woods to get the logs and sticks. So, I made do with a small amount that I'd found nearby. I used a blank page from my journal and used the multi tool to shred some sticks to use as kindling and used my cigarette lighter to set it all alight. I then placed a small pile of sticks and wood chips that I'd accumulated over the small smouldering fire and before I knew it, it was all ablaze.

I sat under a large tree with my back against the trunk, staring into the surrounding darkness with only the moon and stars lighting up the distance. I drifted off to sleep after an hour of sitting down. The long days of hiking, sleepless nights and exhaustion had taken its toll and so I essentially passed out. This was a horrible thing to have happened because I woke up with a shock to find that it was snowing hard, my fire had gone out and I was freezing cold in the encapsulating blackness of night. But what made it even worse was that I wasn't alone. I could hear the familiar cracking of branches, the horrifying huffs and the gargantuan grunts of the beast as the moon cast shadows amongst the trees on Saint Severn. I had no idea at the time how it kept finding me, but I knew it was hunting me. I tried hard to relight the fire, knowing that the monster hated the flames before but there was no hope of that happening, my entire campfire was buried under the heavy falling snow. My only options were to either hide or to run and since the latter would have been a challenge even without a predator hunting me, I decided the best thing for me to do was to hide.

I was unsure of whether or not to cover myself in snow or climb a tree. I knew the risk of hyperthermia and frostbite would be astronomical if I covered myself in snow so decided that climbing a tree would be the smarter choice. Luckily, there was one very close by that was easily scalable, even with a damaged leg. I dropped my makeshift walking stick and began to climb as high and as fast as I could whilst the sound of booming footsteps got sickeningly nearby. Every branch I climbed was covered in mounds of fluffy, fresh snow that crumbled and fell as I put my weight on them. I finally got to a clear part of the tree, fairly high off the ground and sat between a split in the trunk about 20 feet up. I felt safe for all of 3 or 4 seconds, because as soon as I thought I'd hidden from my hunter, I heard the footsteps stop directly underneath me. Even though I was 20 feet in the air, I could still hear its heavy breathing the sound of it searching for my scent as its gigantic nostrils sniffed the air. That was when the nightmare truly began.

First, I stayed as quiet as can be, even held my hand over my mouth to eliminate any potential of inadvertent sounds escaping. But just as I did this, there was a slight thud on the tree, causing it to vibrate slightly. Then it was a continuous and aggressive shake causing the snow to fall off the branches above and below me. This was followed by the unmistakable gurgling growls of the beast below. I held on to the trunk so very tightly and closed my eyes hoping that it would lose interest and just go away. Then, as if my wish was granted, it all stopped. I couldn't hear anything. The tree stopped shaking and the growling had ceased. I opened my eyes, and scanned the darkness around the other trees, but saw no movement at all. I felt relieved. I felt like I'd actually successfully hidden from the beast, and it was moving on, that was until I looked directly down toward the base of the tree I was sat in, in that very instant my heart jumped into my throat and stomach flipped upside down. Because this beast was still there. Gazing up at me with its cold, dead eyes and its hideously large, toothy mouth agape whilst its long, thick tongue hung out of the side. It just stood there, gripping the tree and silently staring at me.

In a flash I felt all the relief, miniscule as it was, disperse from my body as if it was a physical reaction to fear. I was so frightened, but I was also in incomprehensible pain, I was exhausted and so frustrated that the combination of everything just made me feel incredibly angry. So, I felt compelled to shout at the beast. I screamed "what do you want?" and "leave me alone!" at the top of my lungs but to no avail. I wasn't anticipating a reply from the thing, but I was hoping it would scare it and it would run. It's funny to me now that I think of it. I was hiding up a tree, shaking like a leaf in a heavy breeze and stuttering out some warbling wails in hopes of scaring off this colossal animal in its own house. It was stupid and, needless to say, ineffective. But it was all I had. It just kept on staring at me. The snow had stopped, and the moon had fully broken through the clouds. The brighter it got, the more detail I could see on the thing. From blood stains in every shade of red all over its fur, its cracked blueish grey skin on its face and chest, I could see the glint in it's one good eye and, for that matter, the lack of any shine from the other. I thought that if I could tough out the cold and wait it out, then maybe it would leave come the dawn.

I sat there staring at it for what felt like hours and the only movement it made was a slight head tilt and moving its tongue. It had the foulest odour emitting

from it, reminiscent of the rotten scent of

decomposition. It was enough to make anyone feel

nauseous. I took my eyes off of it for a moment as I

heard an owl screech nearby and when I quickly darted

my eyes back down, the beast was gone. I quickly shot

my eyes around looking for it when all of a sudden, I

heard the unforgettable sound of its roar. A loud, ear-

splitting scream descending into a gravelly grumble of a

growl. I thought for a second that it had finally lost

interest until what followed were loud galloping sounds,

I saw it bounding across the open plains running almost

like a big cat, it crashed into the tree I was in so hard

that it snapped and was about to come crashing down,

so I quickly got up on instinct and attempted to jump to the next tree.

I took a leap of faith and as I jumped, I felt the icy cold wind fill my lungs and every hair on my body stood on end. Everything felt like slow motion, until I realised that I had severely overestimated my leaping abilities and ended up grabbing onto a branch around 12 feet off the ground, which promptly snapped, sending me back first into the snowy ground below. I hit the ground with a thump as all that icy cold air shot out from my lungs. I gasped for air and got straight back up, covered in snow, with a now severely swollen and possibly fractured leg and only the moonlight giving me a sense of whereabouts, I knew I had no time to feel the fall I'd just taken. So, I walked backwards a few steps and saw

a giant silhouetted shape dart behind some trees in

front of me. At this stage, I knew I was going to be

attacked again but I remembered I had the multi tool in

my pocket. It had a ruler, some screw drivers, a small

knife, a nail file and a corkscrew on it. I chose the

corkscrew, holding it in my hand and placing the spike

of the corkscrew between my ring and middle fingers,

so it protruded outwards as I formed a fist. I felt like I

was ready to defend myself and knew it was either me

or the beast.

But for such a large, lumbering beast, it could move

with precision. Almost as if it had mastered the art of

stealth. I never saw it move from behind the tree it

went behind, but somehow it had gotten to the right side of me and it just hit me like a bulldozer and pinned me to the ground. This time though, it was angry. It bit me on the arm within seconds of being on me. Its giant jagged jaws plunged deep into my bicep, I felt it's tusks pierce my skin, flesh, muscle and eventually collide with my bone sending an electric like jolt to my brain. The bone stood no chance against the bite force of this beast. My arm instantly snapped like a toothpick, and I could hear a scream in the distance. I thought for a moment that someone else was there, screaming and coming to help me, until I realised it was the sound of my own scream echoing around the vast, dark emptiness of the Saint Severn Mountain.

Not only did I realise in this moment that I was alone and that this monstrous maneater was more than likely about to kill me, but I also felt incredible sadness, pain and fear. Which apparently is an adrenaline filled concoction for survival and pure rage, because I somehow stood up and punched the beast in its side and it's arms using the corkscrew and burning up every single ounce of strength I had left in me. It let go of my arm at this point and knocked me down in one swipe of its mighty hand. It stood there staring at me for a few seconds, almost as if it was acknowledging the fight, I had in me and weighing up if I was worth it. It stomped over to me and slowly stood on my injured leg, I let out a loud scream again as I felt the bone crunch for sure this time and it placed its large, leathery skinned hand around my throat. It took its foot off of my leg and picked me up by my throat, leaving my leg lifeless and dangling and my arm broken and bleeding profusely. It then brought me in so close that I was literally face to face with this immense being. The smell was unbearable, the feel of its moist and foul breath on my face was disgusting. I was in so much pain that I almost just wanted him to end my life. "Just end it all now" I thought. But it didn't. It just stared at me. Just as my oxygen was running out in its vice like choke and visions of my childhood raced through my mind, I raised my hand in one final attempt to survive. I went to punch the thing in its one good eye with the corkscrew in my fist, hoping to fully blind it. But I missed and stabbed it in the nose instead, which worked just as well because it released me.

I dragged myself over to my bag, gasping for air, leaving a trail of blood from my arm behind me. I reached the backpack, quickly untied it with my one good one hand and my teeth. The beast roared in pain in the background and all I could grab was my lighter, I rolled over and grabbed a stick from the fallen tree, but I had no way of lighting it as it was slightly damp from the snow it had fallen into. I lost all hope as the beast stopped its hollering and stared at me again with its remaining vacant white eye and now bleeding from its nose. As it took a step toward me, my world turned once more into a flash of me being a kid and going on hikes with my older brother, then to my 10th Christmas

when I got my first set of hiking boots, then to school

where I met my best friends. My mind was cast to The

Jumping Jack with everyone, Gerry, Lacey, Ron, we'd all

been friends for almost my entire life and then my

thoughts turned to Tina and how I should have taken

my shot with her years ago, how I should have listened

to her and stayed home, how I wanted nothing more

than to be with her in this very moment, what very well

could have been my final moment. But then it clicked.

She left me the note. I put the note in my breast pocket

under my coat. I snapped out of my thoughts and

frantically unzipped my coat with my one good arm. The

beast was taking its time stalking ever so slowly up to

me, almost as if it was smug in the knowledge that it

had me on a figurative silver platter. I reached inside my coat and there it was, the note from Tina. "Please don't die. X" it read, and I almost smiled through the agony because it gave me all the motivation I needed. I put the note between my teeth, sparked the lighter and lit the note on fire, singeing my beard and burning my nose in the process but I didn't care. The beast took a step back when it saw the flickers of flame near my mouth, and it stood very still for a moment. I then quickly threw my plastic lighter on the ground and stabbed it with the stick, shattering it and covering it in lighter fluid. I brought the stick up to my face with a mouthful of flames and the accelerant worked. It was finally aflame.

The beast stood still, staring at me as I spat the charred note out of my mouth and brandished a flaming stick. Which sounds great, but I was also laying on the ground half dead. I must have looked like such easy prey by now, bleeding and groaning in merciless pain, but once again, to my amazement, the giant monster scarpered. Running away from the sight of fire. I didn't hesitate to roll and grab as many sticks as I could, rubbing them in the lighter fluid soaked snow and placing the lit stick on top. I finally had a fire. I quickly went into my bag again and retrieved the bandages I'd gotten earlier. I wrapped my arm up, tight and using both rolls of bandages, however the blood had soaked through them all within 5 minutes. I knew I was in deep trouble and needed some help or I would die out here in a matter of hours.

When daylight broke, it was like a beacon of hope. I had

an opportunity to make it back that day or die that night

and I planned on the former. So, I made the ever so

painful crawl over to where the tree I was hiding in was

knocked down, found and picked up my sturdy walking

stick and proceeded to hop downhill for hours. I didn't

even stop to take a drink. I just hopped and hopped.

Regardless of the pain, I needed to get home. I must

have done at least 6 miles in 8 hours. I was getting

closer and closer. I was relentless. Ignoring my broken

arm and leg in favour of getting home. I got to the large

hill that I had climbed, where the "shortcut" was, and

the bear was decimated. I didn't turn to look, I just

walked on by. That was until a large wooden log flew

past my head and landed on the ground in front of me. It startled me, so I turned around to see exactly what I had feared, although in the back of my mind I knew immediately what I would see anyway. The beast, in broad daylight. Standing in the entrance of the 'shortcut'. Angry. Panting. Snarling. Saliva dripping and oozing from its mouth. It's hands and fingers stretching outward and clenching together over and over. It's yellowed teeth and tusks almost glistening in the sunlight. I could see it's muscular frame, as its muscles rippled under the thick white fur that was stained with aged blood.

I turned and tried to get down the 75 foot hill without it getting close to me, but that was never going to happen. It made a singular leap and got me, only this time it went straight for my head. It slammed me down into the snow and just started savaging me. Ripping my hair out in chunks and scratching my scalp until I felt it clamp its razor sharp teeth down into my head. I could hear and feel the teeth scraping against my skull and suddenly wondered why I had a mouthful of sand in a snowy mountain range, then I realised it wasn't sand at all, it was my cracked and broken teeth. I was so close to the end, I thought I was going to make it home. But unfortunately, the beast had other plans. It clamped it's gargantuan jaws around my cranium and took a hefty chunk of my scalp with it as it ripped my head open, leaving me seeing nothing but deep dark red as the blood soaked into my eyes. It then plunged it's twisted tusks into my shoulder, hoisted me up and threw me like a used toy about 20 feet down the hill. I rolled about another 30 feet or so leaving a spattering of clumpy crimson snow behind me as I tumbled. At that moment I was seeing nothing but bright lights with darkness around my periphery. I thought it was my time to die, that's when everything around me faded to black.

I can remember waking up for a few seconds and hearing an echoed shout off in the distance, but then I drifted back out of consciousness soon after. It felt like a long sleep, but I slipped back into being awake and heard the shouting again, only this time much louder. "Hello!" the disembodied voice said. I truly wasn't sure if I was alive and hallucinating or dead and entering the afterlife, but I couldn't lift my body, or move my head, my arms weren't working, and my right leg was already broken. All I had was my one good leg, which I lifted up and slammed into the ground with all of the remaining force that I had left in reserve and in that instant, I heard the faceless voice say something that I will remember until my dying breath; "Holy shit, bro! He's still alive!".

The next few hours are a bit of a blur. But it comes back to me in flashes, almost like a highlight reel of sorts. I remember seeing a smiling man looking down at me and telling me everything was going to be okay. I also vividly remember the look of horror on his friend's face as he looked at me too. Before I went unconscious again, I heard the crackling static sound of a radio and the smiling man's voice exclaiming that they needed immediate assistance, then it all went black again. Next thing I recall is a blanket being placed on me and I heard the whirring sound of a helicopter in the distance. I then closed my eyes for what felt like a few seconds before being awoken by a jovial woman wearing sunglasses and a very bright air ambulance jacket strapping me to a board and telling me I was going for a helicopter ride. I think I may have even smiled at this news as I'd always wanted to go on a Helicopter, but they gave me so many drugs that I don't even remember getting on the chopper at all. My next flash of memory is full of speeding lights on a cream coloured ceiling and lots of loud chatter as I was being wheeled down a hospital corridor on a gurney.

After this, my memory is concrete. But that isn't as positive as you might think. Because when I woke up, I was back on the Mountain and face to face with the beast again. I had to experience the pain of being torn apart, having my limbs shattered and my head being slowly crushed over and over for what felt like an eternity and I felt all of it. But then, out of nowhere, I woke up. I was in a hospital bed surrounded by nurses and doctors. I was so confused and terrified that the beast was about to return to end me, but the nurses surrounded me and assured me that everything was okay and that I was now safe. They told me I was in hospital and that I had suffered a multitude of very serious injuries. I was panicking and about to freak out but then the door to my room swung open and in ran the only person in the world that I'd wanted to see. Tina.

The nurses all stepped back as Tina burst past them in tears. She bent over my bed and kissed me about 20 times on the lips, they all hurt but I didn't care one bit. All my worries vanished the second I saw her. "You stupid, stupid man!" I remember her saying as she kissed me again. I could taste the saltiness of her tears that had streamed down to her lips on that one. "I told you not to go alone. I told you!" She said whilst staring at me with wild eyes. "We almost lost you. I almost lost you, Al." she said in a sort of squeak. I didn't know what to say, I had no words. Tina looked up at me with a sorrowful smirk and said "but trust you to try to take on a freaking bear though, huh?". I loudly said "no." but she shushed me and told me to save my strength for healing. But I ignored the advice and just about forced out the words "It wasn't a bear". She looked puzzled for a moment but then smiled and said "Okay. Just relax now and we'll talk about it later.". I repeated "it wasn't a bear" a few more times before involuntarily drifting back to sleep.

When I woke up, Tina was still there, only now she was joined by my mom and Dad, my brother and my group of friends Gerry, Lacey and Ron. There were so many gifts and flowers, chocolates and my favourite donuts.

They all smiled when I woke up. I felt a lot more rested

this time around and had a lot more of my bearings. I

looked at them all and said "Wow. Is it my birthday or

something?" The room filled with relieved laughter and

Gerry added that he was glad I hadn't lost my sense of

humour because he had a little something for me as he

pulled out a gigantic Teddy bear and said "this one

won't put up such a fight!" Everyone burst out laughing,

everyone but me. My face dropped and I frowned at the

big stuffed toy. The laughing stopped instantly as if

someone had pressed a 'mute' button on a remote. "I'm

so sorry, Al. I didn't think. It was a stupid idea." Gerry

said with a shaky tone, but I shook my head and said

"it's not that, Gerry. It wasn't a bear that got me. I told

Tina that.". Everyone looked at one another in confusion. Tina came to me and said she thought I was just in shock and the drugs were making me talk funny, but I assured her that what had attacked me was not a bear. Lacey asked me what it was and if I could tell them what had happened. I told them all that I could recall in that moment. The height, the fur, the tusks, the way it moved, the way it pulverised the grizzly bear, its hands, its ghostly white yet ironically cavernous eyes and its hellish roar.

My Dad was, unsurprisingly, the first to dismiss it. He told me I was cold, hungry, hurt, in a new environment and that I was obviously confused about what had happened. But I told him he was wrong, so he shook his head and put his hands in his pockets, which was my dad's way of saying that he was done with the conversation. My Mum said that there was a chance I was mistaken given the amount of trauma I'd gone through. I began to get agitated and some of my machines began to beep behind me which caused my friends and family to step backwards as some nurses came in and asked everyone to please leave. Tina refused and asked if she could stay, the Nurses looked at me and I requested that Tina stayed too, so the nurses agreed and asked everyone else to leave. They all told me they loved me, and they'd see me soon. Tina gave them all a hug and shut the door behind them.

The nurses stayed to stop the beeping and ask me some questions about how I was feeling, then they told me a doctor would come by to see me later and explain everything that had happened. Once they'd left, Tina and I were in the room alone. I looked over at Tina who was staring at me and biting her lip, her eyes were full of tears and quickly darting side to side as she studied my face. "I believe you." she said. I breathed a heavy sigh of relief as she explained that she knows me better than anyone and knows that I wouldn't lie or make something up like this and how I know wildlife better than anyone she's ever known, she ended with "Honey, if you say it wasn't a bear, then it wasn't a god damn bear.". It made me smile and it was then that I knew she had my back in this, even if no one else did.

We spent the next hour just holding hands and talking about what had happened. So much came flooding back and I explained to her how the note she left on my car saved my life during the second attack and that she was all that was on my mind in what I believed to be my final moments. She cried and told me that when she'd heard I was in hospital in critical condition, she couldn't handle the thought of living a life without me in it. She told me that she wasn't holding back anything anymore and that she'd been hiding it away for too long in fear of losing me as her best friend. That was when she told me she loved me and that she'd loved me for the better part of 5 years. I told her that I'd always had a crush on her but had felt the same way for almost the she amount of time, hiding it away for the same reasons she had. We laughed and grinned like idiots. Tina slowly moved closer to me, and we kissed passionately, ignoring the pain until her nose crossed mine and I shuddered a little, she stopped and apologised, we laughed and just continued on kissing for a moment when the doctor walked in and said "Excuse me folks, this is hospital. Not a movie theatre." we stopped and shared a laugh with the doctor who introduced herself to us. "I'm Doctor Waters, it's nice to finally meet you whilst you're awake. We have a lot to go over so I'm glad you have someone here with you because this can be very emotional for some people." she told me. I furled my brow inquisitively and looked at Tina who was looking at me with clamped lips and tears in her eyes. I knew it was bad, but just how bad I wasn't prepared for, but I knew it wasn't going to be anywhere near as bad as dying on that Mountain alone. "Lay it on me, Doc" I said listening intently.

The doctor ran down all of my injuries that I came in with. My left tibia and fibula in my lower leg had been broken in 6 places, the metatarsals in my left foot had all been crushes into pieces too, due to this I couldn't feel the frostbite setting in to my toes and foot which was irreversible and they had to amputate all of my toes on that foot and some flesh around the area. My clavicle or 'collar bone' had been fractured and I had haemorrhaging from multiple internal wounds in my ribs and stomach area. I had also sustained multiple skull punctures, a broken orbital bone and 8 teeth were cracked and broken. The skull injuries had caused some swelling on my brain but nothing too severe in that regard, despite losing a small piece of my scalp, leaving a small portion of my skull exposed. However, the worst part, yes it gets worse, was my arm. It essentially ripped out my bicep muscle and broke my humerus in 3 places. Also causing severe haemorrhaging. They said that the bandages I'd applied had essentially acted as a tourniquet and slowed the bleeding just enough to ensure that I didn't bleed out, but in doing so I had permanently damaged the nerves in my arm, Dr Waters told me that my arm would never return to full functionality ever again and that my climbing ventures were almost certainly over for good. They needed to do

8 surgeries that accumulated to 22 hours in total. On top of all of this, due to the severity of my injuries, I needed to be placed in an induced coma and was in that coma for just over 4 weeks. Which was a shock to me because I thought only a few days had passed at that point. Because of this, the muscles in my legs had deteriorated and I would essentially need to learn to walk again in order to strengthen them up. I had a long road ahead of me and just as I felt the weight of all the information crushing me, Tina's hand gripped mine tightly and she said "We will get through this. Together.".

Dr Waters told me that this was the worst bear attack they'd ever seen. I told her that it wasn't a bear, it was something I'd never seen before, but she then told me that all of my injuries are consistent with bear attacks, albeit many different ones amalgamated and possibly one of the biggest bears on record given the bite radius. She then told me that it is her professional opinion that I was attacked by the bear, I lost blood and had a severe head injury and therefore became delirious and unaware of what was happening. The snow covered bear caused me to see something that wasn't there. I told her that it was my professional opinion that she was full of shit and wasn't there to experience it like I was. Tina gripped my hand tighter and apologised to the Doctor for my outburst, the Doctor smiled and said it was quite okay and that its normal to feel like this after such a traumatic experience and a hard conversation.

The Doctor left and all I felt was deep anger and like I was a child telling their parents about the monster under their bed.

After 2 more days, the police stopped by as I'd mentioned the remains of Maggie's parents in the rainbow tent. I told them what happened, and Tina handed them the bloodstained photograph that I'd brought back with me to return to Maggie. They thanked me and left. 4 days later, they'd found them, and it was on the news that a bear had attacked and killed a couple in the Severn Mountains, but their bodies were never recovered. I was infuriated that they blamed a bear for that much devastation. I felt like everyone was playing dumb for whatever reason, but then I remembered that this thing had never been seen before. So, imagining it would be like imagining a brand new colour, which is impossible. But it was still getting me very upset that no one believed my story except for Tina.

3 more weeks flew by, and I was able to leave the hospital and go home. About a week prior, we had agreed that Tina would move her stuff into my place whilst I was in hospital, and she would move in with me to "help with my recovery". We both knew it wasn't just for that reason though. It took no time to adjust to it because it just felt right. She was there for me through it all. Even the nightmares and flashbacks where I'd experience the attack all over again and wake up in

pools of sweat every night for weeks. Within 4 months I was walking again, with crutches and I needed a wheelchair for any long journeys, but I was so proud of my achievement. Tina and I were stronger than ever after 6 months and I was head over heels in love so I asked her to marry me, to which she said yes without hesitation. Our friends were elated for us, and I asked Gerry and Ron to be my Best Men and Tina asked Lacey to be Maid of Honour. 2 months later, we were married in a church surrounded by all of our friends and family, and I even walked unassisted for the first time since the attack to take my bride's hand at the altar.

After another 3 months of happy marriage, I decided to go public with my story and reach out to the papers and news outlets. I told them what had happened to me, including what I'd found in the rainbow tent and every paper and news channel reported on it, at first it was taken seriously, and they even had a team of hunters and professional climbers go looking for the beast, but they never found it. No tracks. No fur. Nothing. However, they did find something. My lucky blanket, high up in the trees near the entrance to the "shortcut", how it got up there I don't know, but I have an idea. They returned it to me, weather beaten and ripped, stained with a plethora of colours and smelling like a wet dog. It looked about as rough as I did. But all things considered, getting it back felt like a victory.

Once the journalists had reached out to Dr Waters and the hospital for a comment though everything changed. She was still putting her whole reputation and stock into it being a bear attack and once she had given the media that, it was like a nail in the coffin of the truth. After that, the news reports went from "Man attacked by mystery beast in the Severn Mountains" and "Giant Snow Beast in Severn Mountains says victim!" to "Man Mistakes Bear For Monster, Experts Say" and "Man Misidentifies Snow Covered Bear for Mountain Monster". It was a gut punch, because all of my credibility was gone in the blink of an eye it seemed. Sure, it became local legend around the area and people still talk about it to this day, but I don't. I decided that it was taking too much of my happiness away to defend something that I knew was the truth and that others purely speculated on. It hurt me that people would blindly deny the victim but believe the person who wasn't even there. Even our closest friends stopped talking to me about it because they thought it was "feeding my delusion" as Ron put it once. Which cut deeply.

So, Tina and I moved on, left it in our past and focused on our present and planned for our future. We started a family and had our first child, Cole, in 1991, followed by twin girls Chloe and Georgia in 1993. Needless to say, our hands and our hearts were well and truly full. Lacey and Ron got married in '95 and are still together now, we see them regularly. Gerry got married at 56 years old to his long term boyfriend, Anthony, and they've just celebrated 10 years of marriage too. I'd say I have lived a wonderful life and have been very lucky to have been given a second chance.

Now I'm 67 and it's been 33 years. My kids are all grown up have kids of their own and Tina and I are just as in love as we always have been. Our kids have always remarked at how "sickly sweet" we are together and that we are more like teenagers than they ever were.

Despite everything being close to perfect most of the time, every now and again, just like today, I remember in great detail that cold, dark time in the Saint Severn

Mountain in January of '88. My arm never did regain full functionality, so I guess Dr Waters did get something right. But I work with what I have and I'm still able to do most of the things I want to do. I also say we have moved on, but I'd be lying if I said I didn't still wonder where the beast is today and how no one has found any evidence of it ever being there or even existing, or maybe they have but didn't live to tell the tale like I did. Sometimes I do wonder if it was truly there, but then I snap myself out of it and remember the look in its eyes as it gripped my throat and picked me up, the putrid odour emitting from its mouth filled with rows of teeth and tusks. I've still never seen any mention of the beast in any book I've ever read or in any books on "Cryptids", "Folklore" or "Mythological Beasts" that I've flicked through in a Library or in articles online. But the locals

around the area and some folks on the internet dubbed

it the "Bête De Glace" which is French for "Ice Beast".

Some even call it 'Betty' for short, which is a play on

"Yeti" I guess. It used to make me angry because it was

not a cute, soft little thing like the name "Betty" would

suggest, it was a giant living nightmare that tore me to

pieces. But I don't let it bother me anymore.

So here I am, 67 years young and sat at my writing desk

typing this email out on my PC to a total stranger

because it seemed everything aligned to push me into

doing it. I feel better having written this out though.

Almost like therapy I didn't even know I needed. I hope

it reaches you well, Dr Johnstone and I hope it was what

you were looking for. If not, I still want to thank you for giving me a reason to write it.

Warmest regards,

Albert

Doctor's notes: *This story really took me by surprise. I wasn't expecting anything like this when I initially sent out my advertisements. What Al went through was deeply traumatic both physically and emotionally. I've done hours of research on this story and managed to find copious amounts of videos on the internet of people discussing the 'mystery attack' and using words like 'Legend' and 'Cryptid' when referring to the Bête De Glace but never any footage, photographs or even so much as a sighting report which would make it easy for*

anyone to claim this story is false or even agree with the

Doctors who treated Al. But all anyone has to do is

speak directly to Al about this and their minds will

drastically shift from being unsure to being absolutely

positive that Al's account is 100 percent truth.

I was very fortunate to be able to speak with Al after I'd

received his story. I wrote him back and arranged a

meet up at his home in Shawinigan, Canada. I sat with

him and Tina as we discussed his story over coffee and

cake. Firstly, they were so inexplicably in love and so

sweet together. The kind of love that would give anyone

hope that true love does indeed exist. Secondly, I

couldn't help but get lost in the sincerity of Al's account.

I've never heard anything that, on paper, sounds so farfetched be so impossibly believable and I'm a medium for crying out loud!

This is not one that will ever leave my mind. I will remember Al, Tina and the Bête De Glace for the rest of my days. I truly hope that one day someone manages to prove everyone wrong about Al's account. I know he's not worried about whether or not anyone believes him because he knows what happened was true. But, for me, I want him to get the vindication and recognition that he deserves. He wasn't seen as a survivor of a horrific and terrifying attack that should have killed him. He was painted as a madman. A joke. Which is abhorrent in whatever way you look at it.

Thank you for your story, time, cake and hospitality, Al and Tina. - HJ

Story III – Blue Rock National Park

I'm gonna just jump right in.

My name is Tammy and I have a story not a single soul believes. This happened just 4 years ago.

I had a group of the most amazing friends a person could ask for. I never liked dresses or princesses growing up, always preferred to play soccer and roll around in the dirt finding bugs. Most parents would have forced their kid into a gender norm but not mine. They let me be who I was and never forced me to be anything I wasn't. As a result, I was able to form amazing friendships with people as a kid and remain friends with them for my entire life. 4 in particular were my closest friends. We were all alternative, but I guess for this story's purposes we would be seen by most as "goths" or "emo". We all had black hair with a few hints of bright red or green. I wore all black clothes and big boots. I preferred to have my hair short, but kept it long at the back, kind of like a feathered mullet. My god I was cool, huh? My group of close friends were all dudes. Their names were Gary who was my oldest friend and I affectionately dubbed him "Gar-Bear" on occasion, Dennis, a tall and skinny dude who I'd met in second grade, Bruce who was the oldest of the group by 4 months but you'd think it was 4 years, he was always the "dad" of the group, and then there was Kit, the youngest of the group, a year below us all in school but that didn't matter to us, he was just so funny and chill that we enjoyed his company. As Kit got older, he began playing guitar, had long hair and a beard, always wore flannel and jeans and smoked a lot of weed, as we all did. Bruce was always tall and scrawny as a kid but filled out a lot in his later teens as he was tall and muscular with a head of medium length thick black hair, thick stubble, and a thick handlebar moustache. We always joked and said that he looked like a porn star, but he loved that comparison. Dennis wasn't much shorter than Bruce but was much less muscular and had very thin, blond hair that was clearly balding, but he'd comb his hair over and stick it down with way too much gel to try to hide it. He always had such a genuine spirit and lots of love. Finally, Gary. I met Gary in preschool, and we were practically joined at the hip all through school, everyone said we were either banging each other or he was gay. He was very much gay, but we always liked to keep people guessing and not give them the satisfaction of being "right" about their judgements. He was short, very athletic as he was an outdoor survivalist, he also had long dreadlocks that he wore in a loose bun with a shaggy beard alongside his abundance of facial piercings and tattoos all over his body. These guys all felt like my brothers, they were all older than me by a few months, except Kit who was a year younger than us all, but all four of them were very protective of me, just as I was of them.

For example, when I was 17 I lost my virginity to a guy I'd been dating for a few months who then cheated on me a week later and when the guys found out about it they beat the shit out of him in a mosh pit at a local hardcore show they knew he

was going to be attending. I did not approve, but

that's what they did. They had my back through

everything. We were a group that were constantly

together, mostly all of us, but sometimes it was

different combinations of us, usually only when one

or more of us were grounded. We spent so many

nights camping out in a tent with our parents

thinking we were just camping and telling ghost

stories but actually we were in the middle of a field

getting morbidly drunk and stoned on the cheapest

alcohol and weed we could get our hands on.

Although I do remember one evening when we

actually did stay at Kit's and he said he had a tattoo

machine under his bed that his parents didn't know about, Gary got all excited and wanted a tattoo, so naturally Kit then tattooed a terrible rose design on Gary's chest, but then Gary asked Kit to surround the tattoo with all of our initials right over his heart. He was so proud of it, and it was a really sweet sentiment, but it looked really terrible.

Our teenage years were the best years of my life for a long while. That was until I met Alan. Alan was a geeky kid in school, always into comics and video games, his group of friends stayed inside on hot days and played D&D whilst everyone else went to the beach, house parties and gigs. I met Alan at a

Spider Spawner show in '09 when we were 21. I was

shocked to see him there as I never knew he even

liked music, let alone Norwegian Death Metal. Alan

was far from the spindly, spotty sloth he used to be.

He had become a husky man with long curly hair

and a bushy beard. I told him he reminded me of a

grizzly bear, and he growled at me, which was

simultaneously cringe and incredibly cute but

somehow, I couldn't help but giggle like a smitten

schoolgirl. He and I hit it off and ended up making

out by the end of the 3rd song. I'd like to tell some

romantic story of how we exchanged numbers and

wouldn't stop talking on the phone until the early

hours, courting each other until we met under the

stars in June and made sweet passionate love. But that didn't happen. During the show we snuck off to a port-a-potty and screwed each other's brains out. From then it was pretty heavy and steady. We talked all the time; we were texting all the time and before I knew it Alan quickly became a firm member of our group. The guys were a bit weird about him at first but once they saw how funny and chill he was, not to mention how happy he made me, Alan was accepted with open arms. We dated for 9 years and lived together for 7 of those years before he popped the big question, and I said yes without hesitation. The ring was a white gold band with an onyx stone in the centre, he always knew me so well, and the outside of the ring was surrounded by tiny diamonds to keep some element of tradition alive. The guys were all so excited for us and shrieked when we told them we were getting hitched, the decibel levels they hit were a little bit insane actually. Except for Bruce who had become Alan's best buddy over the last 8 years, so he knew all about it months prior and was asked to be Best Man before Alan had even asked me. We all had a long hug and went out to celebrate hard and old school style. We hit around 11 different bars that night, scoring free drinks from anyone who found out about our engagement. We all got absolutely hammered! It was one of my favourite nights we'd ever shared as a group.

Another year of jokes, drinks, gigs and, of course, being engaged had passed us by when we decided to officially tie the proverbial knot. I asked Gary, Kit and Dennis to be my Bridesmaids and they accepted without even a slight delay. But Kit said, "Only if I can wear a dress, Tam." causing us all to burst out laughing, despite knowing that he probably would wear a dress and look better than me in one too.

After a few months, we were only two weeks away from the wedding and everything had been planned meticulously. I had a big black ball gown; Alan had a

black suit with a red tie. The flowers were black and

red, the tables were black and red, and we even

managed to get our parents to pay for Spider

Spawner to play at the reception as our wedding

band. Which was inexplicably amazing. I didn't plan

on doing a bachelorette party because I didn't like

any girls except my mom and Alan's sister. But Alan

had secretly planned for me and the 4 guys to go on

a camping trip. I was so shocked and asked if he

was coming too but he said "Nope. This is for you

and the guys. You used to go out and get drunk in

the middle of nowhere all the time and I can't think

of a better send off into married life for you than

that." I almost cried when he told me. The guys had planned it all out. They even bought a bunch of stupid bachelorette party sashes, L plates for my shirt and a whole bag of penis shaped straws, whistles, balloons and even a laser pointer. They were just as excited as I was but wouldn't tell me exactly where we were going until the day of the getaway.

Bruce, Kit, Gary and Dennis all stood with me as we got ready. I couldn't believe I was getting married and that a whole trip was planned for me! I couldn't hold it in anymore, so I asked where we were going one last time before Gary sighed, put his arm around me and said "Tammy, we are going to a wonderful place where dreams, wishes and beautiful disasters await." He bent down and stared dramatically into the distance whilst pressing his wiry beard against my face. He continued with a spooky voice "We are going to spend a whole ass weekend in the dreaded Blue Rock National Park" I thought he was kidding as he knew that I'd wanted to go there for the longest time and I hardly ever shut up about it, but the guys all stared at me as I waited for the punchline. But it didn't come. So, I asked "Wait, are you serious?" They all smiled like idiots and nodded emphatically as I hopped up and down with excitement barely containing my squeals. I couldn't believe it. Idaho was a long drive,

but I couldn't wait. Blue Rock was notorious for

supernatural occurrences. Lights in the skies

reported all the time, people disappearing, strange

rock formations appearing out of nowhere

overnight and animal remains found to have been

mutilated beyond recognition were among some of

the many things reported to occur there. This

would usually turn the average person off, but I am

no average person. I was so intensely excited about

going there. I was always fascinated by its history

and the many spooky stories surrounding it.

I had all my stuff packed within 30 minutes, I put

my long black hair in a bun and slid a Spider

Spawner beanie on my head. I was ready to go

make some memories! I kissed Alan goodbye and

told him I loved him and that I would "thank him

really hard" when I got home in 2 days. He smiled,

kissed my head and told me "Be good and keep the

boys out of trouble. Also don't go getting snatched

up by any aliens or ghosts, okay?" I playfully pouted

and said "Fine. No ghosts or aliens."

As I bent to pick my bags up Alan spanked my butt

and said, "Just bring this home in one piece." I

turned to kiss him, and Kit said "Guys, this is low

key turning into a porno. Should we take a seat or

pay some kind of entry fee or?" I slapped his stupid arm for it and he and Dennis chuckled like goofy teenage boys. I gave Alan a peck on the lips as the guys all hugged him goodbye, and Bruce gave him a peck on his cheek. Making us all laugh together one final time before everything changed forever. What I wouldn't give to go back to that day and that moment.

We got outside and threw our stuff into Dennis' bright red 5 seat pickup truck. I called Shotgun and got to sit up front with Dennis for the 10-hour drive. We played road games and some drinking games minus the alcohol, like never have I ever, 20 questions and even a little bit of I Spy. We laughed

and joked. Jammed to our favourite bands and ate

a bunch of candy on the trip there and before we

knew it, we made it to the entrance. A huge

wooden sign, easily 20 foot high, that had many

images carved into it of birds, animals and trees

around the words "Welcome to Blue Rock National

Park". I was practically buzzing with excitement and

intrigue. I couldn't wait to get in there and feel the

energy from the place. We drove in and found our

way around the beaten tracks that lead to a car

park. But instead of parking up there, Dennis took

us off road and began driving on the grass and into

the open fields. We all laughed and asked him if he

was crazy but according to him, he'd read online that no one minded this happening. He must have driven 5 or 6 miles before we stopped off in a spot next to a thick wooded area. "Perfect" Dennis said as he yanked back the handbrake with a click and turned the engine off. I hopped out and smelled the Idaho air that was laden with the scent of nature, Roots, grass, wood, flowers. Everything was so quiet except for the birds. We quickly got the tent up that was honestly more of a circus tent than anything, it was ginormous and even had separate compartments as 'Bedrooms' with their own zipper doors. We unloaded our bags from the car and set up the base for the weekend.

Within minutes we had a fire roaring as the sun was coming down and the stars were just coming into focus as their light broke through the violet and peach hues in the evening sky. We had around 100 beers, 2 bottles of vodka and a bunch of alcopops with us. Kit had also brought some weed with him as a surprise, and we all cheered as he showed us like he was showing us a medal he'd achieved or something. Bruce got out his acoustic guitar and began playing an old western style tune in a mainly minor key, which encompassed the nostalgic feeling we all had in that moment. Just like it always used to be. We all hugged and said how much we loved each other and then, just before I began crying, Kit

showed us the joint he'd rolled and lit it up.

We had a wireless speaker with us so we could play

music, which we did but not obnoxiously loud or

anything. We were respectful of the wildlife and

other people who might have been out there

camping. As the night went on, we smoked, we

drank, we cried, we laughed so much that I felt like I

was going to piss my pants! At one point we were

all singing songs together using the inflatable

penises as pretend microphones. I then stood on

the back of the truck and serenaded Kit with a song

that I'd made up on the spot over what Bruce was

playing on the guitar. I don't recall all the lyrics, but I believe some were "You are so fucking pretty and that's not bullshit, you have a face like a model and an ass that won't quit. Something something something, la la la la.. KIT!" I don't like to brag but I think writing songs might have been my true calling in life.

We toasted marshmallows and smoked some weed. It felt so much like we were kids again that I almost felt like we needed to figure out our stories to tell our parents for when we got home. The stars were finally dazzling and there were no clouds in sight. Thousands of stars lit up the sky and the crescent moon beamed down lighting up the grass and

treeline surrounding us. Towards the end of the

night, we were playing the alcoholic version of

'Never Have I Ever" which is a game in where

someone will say "never have I ever done

something" and if you've done the thing, you drink.

If not, then you don't drink. We went around doing

stupid ones at first to get everyone to drink and get

nice and drunk, "never have I ever breathed." And

"never have I ever gone to a shop" but then after a

while Bruce said "never have I ever been high on a

first date" whilst looking at Kit, we all stared at Kit

as he hesitated, looked at us all, stared back at

Bruce and then drank a shot of Vodka making us all

laugh. He then told the story of how he got high before a date and was so stoned that the girl left, and he just ordered a shit tonne of pancakes and ate them all. We were laughing so hard from the way he told it that our bellies hurt, and I had tears rolling down my face. Then Gary went for one that shut the group up for minute. He said, "Never have I ever jacked off to a picture of Tammy." and they all fucking drank except Gary. I was grossed out and, I guess, a little flattered but also remember laughing it off and saying something like "Ew, dudes. Come on." because it was like being told that my brothers once had the hots for me. They all laughed and said they were 14 or 15 when they used to have crushes on me, which was really weird to hear but it didn't make anything weird as we always did stupid shit like that. Nothing else really happened other than more singing and dancing. It was around 1:30am when I turned in and went to sleep. Gary followed me in, but Kit, Dennis and Bruce stayed up a little later to smoke.

When the morning broke, I could hear the guys outside already. Laughing and joking about the night before and trying to remember some of the stuff they'd done and said in their hungover states. I got up and got dressed into my hiking clothes as I was planning to go hiking into the forests to see some of the rock formations and spooky locations that day. I walked out of the tent to overhear Dennis say, "I was so glad you didn't make anything obvious last night.", then I said "Obvious?" and it scared the absolute shit out of them all. They jumped and said, "Damn it, Tammy." As they all smiled at me. I walked up and Bruce hugged me good morning and lead me to the grill like I was a Duchess or some shit. When I got to the grill I could see and smell the bacon sizzling. I was excited to get some food in my belly after a long night of partying.

The early morning breeze was carrying the scent of

bacon, booze and slight B.O. which wasn't a shock

given how much dancing we did the previous night.

There was a cup of fresh coffee waiting for me

which made my heart flutter. I picked the cup up

like a precious new born, "Going on a trek today,

are we?" Kit said looking at my clothes and I

nodded explaining that I wanted to go to see some

of the locations that have fascinated me for years.

They all agreed to do so. Kit rolled a couple of

joints, and the guys packed a backpack with a whole

bunch of beers. We ate our bacon sandwiches

before heading out into the thick brush across from

our campsite. I had a map of the area in my own

bag, but luckily the trails were easy enough to follow, they had been well broken in it seemed. We walked half a mile in and saw a gigantic stag with monstrous antlers galloping through the trees. It was amazing. We could hear birds in the trees, see the rabbits on the ground and after around 45 minutes of walking through the trees we saw a large stone structure, 7 giant rocks standing in a circular pattern atop a hill in the forest. We walked up to them and were stunned at how perfectly circular the pattern was. There was also a slight humming noise coming from the centre of the stones too which gave most of us chills until Bruce pointed out that there was a plane above us. Gary wanted to move on, so we did, but I could have stayed there forever.

We took some photos on our phones and then decided to move on, but as we did, I noticed a small metal object on the ground under some dry leaves. It had symbols on it that I didn't recognise but I did recognise that it was used to burn candles given the melted wax all over the sides of it. I put it in my bag as a souvenir and we carried on the trail. We walked for another half an hour before deciding to take a break and have a beer. Kit lit one of the joints and passed it to me. We were sharing the smoke when we heard some snapping of branches behind us. We all stopped and looked around us in silence. We heard a crunch again, but it was closer this time and we darted our heads to look in the same area of the woods as a bush began to rustle. "Please don't be a bear" Dennis said as we all shushed him feeling the anticipation reaching boiling point and then we watched as a Beagle burst through the bush and ran towards us. The dog was wagging its tail as we all crouched down to give it pets and love before we heard a whistle, and it went running back towards the bush where a man stood holding a rifle.

The man was wearing dark camouflage clothes. He approached us, and as he got closer, we noticed he was very tall with a silver moustache and long silver locks of hair flowing in the wind. "Howdy there, partners." He said with a smile. "Didn't mean to startle y'all.". We exhaled in unison and told him we thought he was a bear, he laughed at us all and said "ain't no damn bears in these parts, kids. Only birds, Elk, Stag and the occasional pack of Coyotes. Although a few folks have said they've seen wolves and a big cat around here, but I've been huntin' these parts for decades and I ain't never seen nothin' like that." We all felt relieved to know we weren't in immediate danger. We offered him a beer, but he declined very politely and said he needed to stay sharp during his hunt. He then pulled up his belt and said "I suppose y'all are here because of the horror stories surrounding these parts?" We said yes but told him it was also to have a really fun Bachelorette shindig. The man turned away for a second before looking back at us and saying "Just be careful. This place ain't no joke. I don't believe in little green fellers in the sky, but I do believe in the disappearances, and I seen the group of people who come up here some nights in their little robes and chantin' gibberish." I asked what he'd seen, and the man looked me dead in the eyes and said "This place holds some unusual secrets I'm sure but those weird cult followers gave it a real bad name." I wanted to hear more about the cult, but he said he was hunting a buck and needed to move on out. We thanked him and he left us. We all looked at each other, digesting what we had just heard and couldn't help but start chuckling. Not sure if it was the weed or just the ridiculousness of what we had just heard but, either way, I really wish we'd listened.

We continued on our pathway into the forest, marvelling at the giant trees, flowery bushes and various birds we could see in the trees. Gary suddenly stopped and gasped so the rest of us halted and looked around at what he was seeing but saw nothing. Dennis asked "What happened, dude?" to which Bruce said "Did you see a spider?" in a very reductive fashion but then Gary said "I'm not kidding, guys and I don't want to freak you out, but I'm pretty sure I just saw someone watching us and then hide behind a tree when I looked at them." We looked at him, then around us before Kit asked "which tree?", so Gary pointed at a large oak tree in the near distance and Kit decided to waltz on up and check it out as he reached the tree he gasped and screamed "Oh my god!" As a hand reached from behind tree and grabbed him around the throat. We all screamed and yelled as we charged at the tree to defend our friend but as we got there Kit began to laugh, we looked on confused as Kit moved from where he was to show us that the hand around his throat was his own and he'd hidden his elbow behind the tree to make it appear like someone else's hand. We all sighed and playfully shoved him back. "You should have seen your faces!" he just about managed to say through his juvenile laughter. But then a Rabbit hopped out from behind a Bush and made Kit jump out of his skin, causing us all to laugh at him. Gary still insisted that he saw someone watching us, but we managed to convince him that it was most likely just the shadows in the forest playing tricks on him.

We continued on into the woods for around 2 hours, taking photos and posing in silly ways as we always did. We reached a tall tree with the bark stripped off of it from the base to around half way up the trunk. I was in awe of this magnificent test of nature, the sheer size of this tree was insane. But as I walked around the other side, I saw that the tree had been carved into. Various symbols and pictures looked to have been carved and burned into the tree, the imagery was depicting what looked to be a dissection of a human body. I couldn't read the symbols, but they were the same ones that were on the metal candle burner I had in my bag. I got a very peculiar feeling in my stomach and so I suggested we head back before nightfall to which they all unanimously agreed so we began walking back, taking our time. It was around four and a half hours of photos, reminiscing, smoking and drinking went by when we reached a T like junction on the trail that we hadn't noticed before. Gary and Kit said "I bet if we went this way we would cut the walking time in half." But Dennis disagreed and said we should follow the path we had already taken. I agreed with Dennis, but Kit and Gary were adamant that we were wrong. So, Bruce was the deciding vote, he looked at Gary and Kit and said "I'll take that bet. I bet you both 20 dollars that we get back before you two." To which they gladly accepted with Kit exclaiming "easiest 20 bucks I've ever made." and they began walking their way. I didn't like that we had split up, so I said "Gar-Bear! We really should stay together" But Gary knew the outdoors very well and said "You're just scared you're gonna lose, Tam" so ever the competitive one, I shook my head and told him he'd be shoving his words up his ass. I wasn't too concerned for their safety or anything, I just didn't want to see something cool and have them miss it and vice versa.

Around another hour had passed by when the sun

had all but set, we could see the camp through the treeline ahead of us, Dennis' bright red pickup was easily visible through the trees too as the moon shone down on it like a beacon. I felt immense relief to have made it back, as I was exhausted. I don't know if you've ever been to Blue Rock but it's absolutely huge and walking for almost 8 hours in a day over the various terrains whilst being both drunk and stoned was very taxing. Self-inflicted, sure, but taxing none the less. Once we'd made it back to camp Bruce called out to Gary and Kit but there was no response. He laughed and said "easiest 20 bucks I've ever made!" in a tone that mocked Kit's voice. Dennis looked in the tent for them, in case they were waiting to scare us, but he walked out saying "nope. They're not here." I was worried as it was dark and so I said "what if they got lost? Or hurt?" But Bruce tutted at me, handed me a beer and said "No chance. You know better than anyone that Gary practically lives outdoors in the woods. They'll be fine." Dennis agreed with him and so we lit a fire and drank our beers, cooked some food and watched the treeline for any sign of Gary or Kit. I tried calling them, but I had no cell service. I noticed both Dennis and Bruce tried calling too but they also said they had no service. The two guys were getting increasingly anxious and concerned as the hours rolled on. It was around 10pm when

Bruce abruptly said "Well, shit. We have to go find them." But it was pitch black out there. I suggested that we all use the torches on our phones, which was agreed by Dennis and Bruce but then as we went to leave, we also decided that Dennis should stay behind in case Gary and Kit come back, he gladly welcomed that suggestion as he didn't want to go wandering around in the woods at night. Who could blame him really? But at this stage we had no choice, we had to find our friends. So, Bruce and I set off into the darkness.

We stepped into the trees and immediately got hit with an increase in humidity, the air was thick, and the insects were out in full force. We heard crickets all over and saw fireflies floating around above us. We shone our phone lights over the rocky areas and trees, noticing some large spiders scuttling away as the light hit them. We then promptly noticed that we still had no cell service but didn't think much of it as we could still use our torches. We called out over and over for them but heard no response. I was getting really scared for their safety and was close to tears when Bruce shushed me and said "Listen", so we listened and heard someone shouting "help" in the distance. We began running and calling out again as the cries for aid got louder and closer. I was so focused on finding the voice calling to us that I tripped over multiple times and cut my leg a little bit and my hands and arms got scuffed and scraped all over by the tree trunks and branches I was rushing through. Bruce ran on a little and reached a ridge with a 20 foot sheer drop. "Is there anyone down there?" He shouted causing his words to echo off of the steep rocky ridge. We heard no response. We discussed the voice calling to us and agreed that it didn't sound like either Gary or Kit. The voice sounded more feminine and wasn't responding to us anymore. We waited in silence for a few moments, crouched down, listening out for any more shouting before we heard a crackle in the bushes. I sprung up and screamed thinking something was behind us, but it was just a pinecone falling from the tree behind us. I sighed in relief and Bruce laughed at me, so I told him to shut up and suggested we head back to camp in case they'd made it back already. Bruce agreed, so we set off back towards camp. Just before we reached the campsite, I experience a very high pitched ring in my ears and they'd also popped and felt like they were full of water. I put my hands to my ears and let out an audible sound of pain and looked at Bruce who was curiously experiencing the same thing I was. We decided to keep walking, but the ground felt steeper than it was before. Our legs were straining, and we were out of breath as we reached the edge of the treeline, once we broke through the trees and into the camp, our ears became clear, and the incessant ringing stopped instantly. I looked at Bruce, he looked back at me and said "That was weird." Which it was but we agreed that it was some kind of large animal deterrent put in by the Park Rangers or something.

We walked over to the camp expecting to see Kit and Gary telling Dennis the story of their epic adventure through the dark woods, but they weren't there, and neither was Dennis. Bruce called out to Dennis but got no response. I said that maybe he just needed to go to the bathroom but then Bruce walked to the other side of the fire and knelt down. He stood up and in his hands were Dennis' cell phone and a half empty can of beer. He gave me the phone and I checked it, but just like ours his cell service wasn't active. I looked up just over the top of the phone and noticed something even more bizarre. Dennis' clothes that he'd been wearing that day were in a heap on the floor. I walked over, picked them up and showed Bruce who then frowned and said "So, Dennis is off running around buck ass naked in the dark with no phone and no light?" I nodded slowly in wide eyed disbelief. Bruce then said "He might have changed clothes after we left and didn't pick them up" I agreed until Bruce said "But let's be real. Either he ate some funky mushrooms, or he's lost his damn mind." I asked him what we should do but he said "You sit tight. I'm going to find him. He can't be that far away." just as he said this an ominous roar of thunder rumbled above and rain began to fall. So, I gathered the electronics, some beers and Dennis' clothes and went inside the tent, sitting just inside the door to the tent looking out into the rainy dark and watching Bruce disappear into the distance. I looked at my phone, I just wanted to call Alan, but I still had no reception. It was around 10 minutes later, I was drinking a beer and smoking a left over cigarette from one of Kit's packs when a rumble

was heard above me but it was distinctly not like

any thunder I'd ever heard. But a loud and high

pitched rumble that gently vibrated the ground. I

looked outside and saw 10 bright blue lights in the

sky above our camp. All in a neat circle and

hovering very still. I dove to get my phone and get

this on camera but as soon as I arrived back to the

entrance, the lights had vanished.

"Holy fucking shit! What on earth did I just see?" I

asked myself over and over. Then it hit me. "The

guys are playing a prank on me. Just like the old

days." I said out loud. My mind turned the cogs and

unravelled their plans. We split up, then they had all periodically disappeared conveniently in the spooky woods where people allegedly disappear all the time, now Bruce has gone to "search for naked Dennis", and I conveniently see lights in the sky "which was probably just some fancy projector shit that Gary got from the Internet." I thought. I laughed to myself "I bet they've got a secret second camp somewhere and have set up this elaborate plan to scare me. "Won't work" I said to myself, and I shook my head, laughed through my nose and stood up. I put on my raincoat and decided to follow the path of Bruce's foot print indents in the long, sodden grass. Once I reached the trees leading into the forest, I began feeling queasy, I ignored it,

thinking I was just hungry and needed to eat, so I

pressed on through the trees until Bruce's tracks

just stopped dead. I looked around but didn't see

them leading anywhere. It looked like he had just

taken off and flew away. My confusion was only

made more severe when I noticed that Bruce's

clothes were in a heap just to the right of where his

tracks stopped. I was confused at this stage as I

didn't know where to go and finding more clothes

meant two of my best friends are running around

naked in the woods at night. I was beginning to

question their choices when a flash of lightning

blasted above me and lit up the forest ahead. It was

then that I saw something run through the trees, it looked like a naked man, so I figured it was probably one of the two. So, I called out for Bruce and Dennis, I told them to stop as I'd figured out the plan. I laughed to myself as I said "May as well call me Detective Tam". All I could hear was the snapping of twigs in the distance. I remember walking forward very slowly and saying something along the lines of "I really don't want to see your dicks flopping around, so if you could cut this shit out and put some pants on that would be very much appreciated." but again, I had no response. I could hear some heavy wheezing breaths and almost like a snorting sound coming from just in front of me. I could see a silhouette of someone

stood ahead of me but the second I shine my light

on them they ran away again. It looked like Bruce,

so I followed and ran after him, jumping over rocks

and tree stumps, running through bushes until I

realised that I was much deeper in the woods than I

wanted to be and that I didn't remember which way

I came from. I began to panic and walk back the

way I thought I came, feeling really angry that the

guys would do this to me. Then I heard a voice, the

same voice Bruce and I had heard earlier, calling for

help again. So, I ran towards it and ended up

reaching the cavern we'd found last time. I looked

over the edge and shone my light down, staring and

measuring the distance. I called out and asked if

anyone was down there. After a few moments of

painful silence, I heard a voice say "Yeah. Please

help me!" I looked over the edge again and

immediately felt two large hands on my back shove

me forward causing me to fall.

Luckily it was more of an incredibly steep hill, so I

ended up rolling down the embankment, digging

my nails into the ground as I fell until I hit the

bottom. I looked at my fingers and saw that 3 of my

nails had all but ripped off and were bleeding

profusely, I screamed and looked up to the top of

the hill to see a person in a hooded reddish brown

cloak holding a flame-lit torch and looking down on

me for a few seconds before they turned and

walked away. "You fucking dick wad! Fuck you!

What the fuck!?" I yelled at them but, they'd gone. I

then realised I needed to get out, so I called out for

help and for them to come back but they didn't. I

shouted "asshole!" as loud as I could which made

feel a little better, but I was quickly rooted back in

the very real scenario that I was stuck in the dark on

my own in the woods. The thunder rolled and the

rain got heavier as I went to stand, and I let out a

howl of pain as I tried and failed to get to my feet.

My phone screen was cracked and covered in mud

but still worked, so I shone my phone light on my

leg and saw that my knee had been cut and was a little out of joint. I knew what to do, Gary had taught me years before it, I rolled up my shirt from the bottom and put it in my mouth, clamping down as hard as I could, then I sharply pulled and twisted my leg, I heard a popping sound and felt an immeasurable level of pain, I screamed but it was muffled due to the shirt in my mouth and I was then able to bend my leg and stand up. I had lots of sharp pains emanating from my knee, but I could stand and walk. I had realised that this was no joke, but part of me still hoped it was. I called out for my friends again but heard no reply. "This isn't funny anymore." I kept saying, despite knowing that it was pointless. When I looked into a gap between the hill and the wall beside it, it had created a cave-like structure. I was about to head that way to get shelter but then as the lightning flashed, I was faced with a harrowing sight. There were 3 human skulls inside of the cave with human looking bones stuck in the ground in a symmetrical pattern. I fell backwards on my ass and began breathing sharply and quickly. I jumped up and tried to desperately climb the steep incline to get back to the top, but the rain combined with my injured fingers and knee meant I couldn't, I just kept slipping down. I was covered in rain and mud and decided that it was no use. I felt utterly hopeless.

It was quiet, I could hear the thunder rumbling
above and the lightning flashed every so often
illuminating my surroundings and showing me
nothing but dense forest ahead of me and the
skeletal remains behind me. I could hear the rain
drops slapping onto the thick leaves of the trees
around me, the wind blew a mild breeze that
carried the scent of freshly mowed grass. It was
eerie.

Just as the silence worsened the tension in the air
and my eyes focused in on the three skulls laid out
in a line over by the cave, my phone chimed loudly
with my guitar squeal ring tone. Which almost gave

me a heart attack.

I scrabbled around trying to get my phone out of my tight pockets as it kept chiming over and over with messages now that I finally had cell service. When I got it out, I looked at my slightly smashed cell screen and saw I had messages from Kit saying "Lost", "Tam" and "Help", then messages from Gary saying "Kit's hurt. We need help!" Then "Please hurry. There's someone watching us." I didn't know what to do but I then got a notification that I had a voicemail from Gary. So, I clicked it and listened, it was mostly static and crackling noises, but I could also hear the faint sound of chanting in the background and then Gary's voice whispered into the phone "Please send some help. I'm pretty sure we're at those weird stones we found earlier." followed by sounds of footsteps approaching him and Gary pleading and screaming "no, please." as his voice got gradually quieter and the phone cut out. I was left shaking after hearing that. I went to call Alan once more, but my service had gone again. I screamed in frustration as I was scared, angry and wondered what had become of my dearest friends. I sat for a moment before I stood up, ignoring any pain and decided I needed to get help to find my friends but first I had to climb back up.

So, I found two very sturdy branches on the ground underneath a large tree and shoved them into the wet mud covering the hill I'd fallen down. I then used these as spikes to drive into each step to ensure I didn't fall again. Another thing Gary told us years prior, and it worked. I made it back to the top. I felt out of breath, but I didn't stop moving once I'd reached the top. I knew someone was out there to hurt me and so I just continued through the forest, trying to recall the directions Bruce and I took last time. I heard noises and what sounded like whispers in the distance, but I didn't see anything. I stopped for a moment to survey the surroundings and see if I was going the right way, but then I heard something drop to the floor and make a

breathy chirping sound. But not like a sound a bird

would make, this was something else. I heard

rustling of leaves and foliage on the ground before

hearing footsteps approaching me. I turned and ran

as fast as I could in the direction that I believed was

right. But it was still so dark, and everything looked

the same. My knee was screaming in pain, but I

tried to ignore it until I tripped on a tree stump and

landed directly on my knee cap. I screamed so loud

that I had to cover my own mouth and bite down

on my finger in order to suppress the sound and the

pain. I quickly looked behind me and noticed that

the footsteps had ceased and that it was very quiet.

That was when I noticed the large stone formation

in the dark just to my right.

I got up to run again but as soon as I did, a flame

torch appeared over one of the rocks. I turn to run

another way and another torch appears and this

continued until I was surrounded by a large circle of

torches. The air became thin, and I found it tough

to breath, I was so scared to move, then the people

holding the torches came into focus. All wearing

blue and white robes with a strange black and gold

logo on the front and back. They were all

whispering to each other so loudly that they

sounded like crickets. They all looked normal, like

anyone you'd see on the street at any time. They took their hoods down revealing that they were all different genders and looked pretty much like regular people except for the wide eyed distant stare they all had. Then half of them began humming and the other half began chanting a phrase that I couldn't make out but sounded like "Erase-Youth-Flow" over and over in the same tone, I noticed that their eyes had rolled back and some began to bleed from the nose as their chanting got louder and more intense. I was screaming at them to help me and to stop but none of them seemed to even acknowledge me. Then, and I'm aware this sounds absolutely crazy, but in what can only be described as 'a moment of sheer nerve shredding fucking horror' a group of blue lights hovered in the skies above us. I looked up and took a step back as a wide beam of white light shone down onto the ground. I was shaken but not paralysed, I got up and ran as fast as I could. I tried to leave the circle but one of the chanters tried to hold me back and in my moment of panic I just headbutted her in the mouth. Which was a stupid choice because she inadvertently bit my head and made me bleed. But I ran through all the discomfort and hurt I was feeling until I could see our campfire burning in the distance. I ran and ran, didn't even stop or slow down on the steep walk up to the camp. I could finally see Dennis' truck and felt a huge sense of relief. I ran straight to it and got in to drive away and get help, but the keys weren't in the ignition. I swore my ass off in that moment until I realised that Dennis left his clothes and bag behind. They were in the tent, and I figured he would have left his car keys in there. So, I got out and ran to the tent, quickly rifling through his bag but find no keys. Then when I went through his shorts that he'd removed earlier, the familiar jingle of keys gave me butterflies in my tummy, and I screamed "I found them." I could have cried I was so relieved. I slowed down and realised that I could taste the blood from my head wound trickling into my mouth and my sweat was dripping into the wound causing it to

sting. I took a few seconds to wipe the blood on my

sleeve before I quickly ran back to the truck. I stuck

the key in the ignition and turned it, but nothing

happened. I tried again but nothing happened

again. I turned it over and over, but nothing

happened. I had a small bit of mechanical

knowledge thanks to my dad, so I jumped out and

popped the hood to see what was wrong and I saw

that the battery wires had been completely

severed. I fell into a sitting position, which was

when I noticed the tyres had also been slashed. I

had no idea what to do next.

I sat for a while. Figuring out what was happening and realising that my friends were actually missing and that I'd really seen the blue lights and the beam and the circle of people chanting and staring. This was no prank. This was no nightmare. It was true, but I didn't understand how or why it was happening. I just hurriedly went into the tent, grabbed a first aid box and patched my head up with a sticky bandage that had a cartoon tiger on it. I wrapped my knee up in a long bandage and ripped holes in 3 socks, slipping them up on my knee to act as a makeshift knee brace. It helped somewhat, but not a great deal. I grabbed my power bank to charge my dirty, cracked phone and started walking into the dark field in search of aid. I knew I had to find help because I knew that even though it was a 6 mile trek in the dark with only a phone flash light and an injured knee, it was a matter of life and death for the guys. My best friends, my brothers, were all missing and I knew that at least one of them was really hurt and in trouble. So, I began the journey. After about a mile and a half I realised that I must have taken a wrong turn, because I wasn't at all where I'd imagined I'd be. Walking in the dark, panicking and injured probably played a big part in that, but the fact is I was lost. The trees were getting thick, the branches were low, and I kept walking into them and getting a face full of cold, wet leaves and sticks. The grass under my feet turned to damp mud and the rain began to fall harder than before. I was about to turn around and go back but then I saw a glimpse of someone running, naked, through the treeline. So, I called out Bruce and Dennis' names in desperation, I quickly picked up the pace and went after them. I'd walked maybe 10 steps into the treeline when I felt the ground give way beneath my feet and at first, I thought I'd walked into a lake or a large puddle, but I knew that there was no water around except the rainfall. I suddenly fell through the ground around 8 feet down and landed on cold stone slabs. I hurt my hands breaking my fall and bashed my knee again on the ground causing me to yell and hear an instant echo surrounding me. I whimpered in pain and clutched my knee before I looked around and gasped. I saw the torches lighting up long stone walkways, twisting all around the place like an underground labyrinth. I cautiously stood up and stumbled into a crooked gait before stumbling forwards to find my way out. I hobbled and walked for around 15 minutes, the walls were crawling with bugs and around every bend there were stone slabs on the walls engraved with strange etchings and imagery. Human body parts lined up next to each other and pregnant women having their babies removed from their wombs all scattered the slabs in the dim, damp tunnels.

Clinging to the dusty walls and holding back my sobs, hiding around every corner and scoping out the place. I concluded that there wasn't anyone there, but I also couldn't find a way out. I hesitantly took a few more turns before coming to a set of 8 stone steps with a large marble archway at the top. There were more etchings on the steps, these ones I did recognise. They were of the logo I'd seen on the robes. A strange overlap of 'V' a smaller 'M' and struck through with a line that had spheres on its ends. I took a deep breath, braced myself and began to walk, slowly, up the steps. Once I made it to the top, I peered through the archway to see more torches, but the corridors veered only left or right and were more of a dirt like substance than stone. Which filled me with relief as I felt like this must have been the exit. It was then that I heard a soft female voice whisper and say "found you".

I turned around sharply to see the same woman I'd headbutted earlier, wild eyed and grinning at me with a missing front tooth and blood stained all over her chin and robe. I stepped back to run when she showed me that she had a large syringe in her hand. I was terrified and decided to disregard all pain, "Just fucking run through the arch way and try to find an exit, Tammy!" my brain was screaming. So, I did. All the while this crazy woman chased me with the needle all around the muddy hallway, laughing with such strain that she sounded like a small child getting tickled.

I was hysterically crying and frantically searching for a way out of this dire situation, when, by the grace of whatever divine entity is above us, I managed to find a hatch in the ceiling with a ladder leading up to it. I was about to climb it but heard the footsteps of the lunatic woman behind me come to halt. I turned and in my tearful rage I said "just fuck off!"

which seemed to just make her giggle even harder, like a straight up maniac. "You have a date." she said whilst chuckling to herself. I told her to back away or I'd kill her which made her laugh even harder. She then stepped forward and I threw my leg outward in an attempt to kick her back, which made this woman jump up and down whilst almost making chimpanzee like sounds. She seemed excited by this, which was extremely unnerving. I turned to run up the ladder, I made it up 4 rungs before I felt the firm grip of her hand around the ankle of my injured leg. I flailed my legs around as she laughed and readied the syringe to plunge it into my skin, but she looked away for a moment and I instantly took the chance to kick her square in the face with my good leg, sending her crumbling to the ground. I didn't hesitate, I just climbed up and opened the hatch. I was in the forest again, amongst the trees but could hear lots of voices and see lots of torches.

I crouched down and hid in amongst some bushes, ignoring the pain in my knee, head and fingers. I went to take my chance to run but just as I went to stand, the woman's head appeared through the hatch, and she screamed like a banshee. Causing all the people to come her, and in doing so, having all the torches shine on her bloodied face. Her mouth was oozing deep red blood and her nose was cut deeply. At that moment she spat the words "She's nearby! Search this area. She's hurt and can't be far. We will please the pure ones this night!". My stomach was vibrating and all the hairs on my body stood up as I heard this.

I waited for my moment and backed away whilst still crouched, I kept my gaze upon their torches as they rummaged around in search of me. I was hit in the head by branches, but I still never took my eyes off of them. I had finally managed to make it to the open fields and decided to make a run for it, I turned from them all and began to gallop like the buck we saw earlier that day, as fast as I possibly could, but then I heard one of them shout "Quick! She's in the open!" and my blood ran cold.

I kept running as the tears streamed from my eyes and the snot mixed with dirt and blood ran into my mouth. I was a mess, but I pressed on with everything I had. I turned around to see 15 or more torch lights emerge from the treeline, hurtling after me. I was so frightened but kept running, I felt myself slowing down which was unusual as I was still putting in all of my efforts to run at a high speed, but all of a sudden, I felt like I was trying to run through waist deep water. I just couldn't gain any momentum. I turned to see the people all stood around 10 feet from me, their eyes shining in their torch lights and their faces barely visible in the darkness. They all looked skyward in unison and then suddenly a bright beam of light hit me from above, the same one as before, but this one felt absolutely freezing cold. I tried to move and get away from it, but I was somehow unable to. I then tried to scream and all that would come out was a light squeak and a whimper. I am not ashamed to say that I was so scared that I pissed myself there and then. All of this was met with a chorus of laughter from the onlookers. I then was lifted into the air very delicately, about 20 feet up as the crowd's laughter turned to cheers and my tears

dripped from my eyes, but instead of dropping,

they floated away from my face, hovering gracefully

and looking like wobbly diamonds in the light

above. I looked down at the crowd to see the

crazed woman that chased me grinning wildly with

her blood soaked face and waving at me before I

got hoisted up even further, around 80 - 100 feet,

at such a high speed that I blacked out.

In an instant, I was back at home. Sat at the dining

table with all of my friends and Alan. Sharing

takeout Mexican food and laughing so hard at

Bruce's jokes. We all clinked our drinks together

and said "to family" with large smiles on our faces. I

felt so relieved to be home with all of my boys. I

was confused but tried desperately to bury all

memory of what had occurred. I delicately caressed

Alan's face and smiled at the feel of his bushy beard

between my fingers. I picked up my burrito, but a

piece fell from it and landed on the floor. Gary

tutted at me and said "Oh trust you to drop food on

the floor, Tam. You hot mess." we all laughed as I

quickly leaned down to grab it from under the table

and when I returned to sitting upright. The guys

were all gone.

I dropped my food on the plate and stood up,

calling for them all. But no one answered. I looked

at the walls and saw they began to melt and sink

into an effervescent mulch on the ground. I ran

around the house trying to find them, but I

couldn't. I went to go upstairs but the stairs were

almost like they were made of water. I couldn't step

on them without sinking into them and feeling the

liquid fill my shoes. I sat down and cried, howling at

the roof as it disintegrated around me. I brought my

thighs into my chest and hugged my knees as I

listened to everything that was familiar dissolve

into nothingness. All I could do was listen as

everything died and when I looked up, I was sat in

my neighbourhood with every house melted down into a bubbling mess of colour. The smell was inexplicable, but it made me want to vomit instantly.

I went to stand up and instantly got pulled back into consciousness. I was laying on a metal slab in a large room with blue and white walls, yellow lights were scattered all over the walls and ceiling and a large mirror hung above me that appeared to be rippling like water. I was breathing heavily and wanted to stand but I couldn't get up. I glanced down to see that, not only was I completely naked, but there was a metallic belt like contraption around my waist keeping me in place. The sense of pure fear I felt in that moment cannot be put into words. They just simply can't. There are no words strong enough.

I tried to push myself out of the belt, but I couldn't. It seemed the harder I tried to get out, the tighter it became so I stopped trying for a moment so I could think of a way out. Which was when I heard a very distorted and shallow breathed voice say "Tammy?" I looked to my left to see Gary laying in a similar fashion to me, totally naked with a metal belt around his waist only he was so pale and the skin on his chest had been removed, leaving nothing but exposed veins, muscle and bone. He smiled at me and said "It'll be okay. Don't worry. We're almost home now."

I could only cry when I saw what had become of my oldest friend. It was as if all the air had been ripped from my lungs. I was stammering and shaking trying to compute what I was seeing in front of me. Through my flood of tears, all I was able to say "I love you, Gar-Bear.", he smiled and closed his eyes. Then his stomach stopped moving up and down and his jaw relaxed. I knew he was gone, and I screamed in disbelief. I fought harder than I've ever fought to get free of the belt holding me down, but then a strange sound came from the ground, a small hatch on the floor at the foot of where Gary laid slid open and the belt holding him in place detached. The metallic platform he was laid upon lifted up vertically and his limp body slid down the metal slab leaving a trail of blood behind him. He disappeared through the chute on the floor before it closed up. I was trying to catch my breath, but I just couldn't. I was in a state of hysteria. I still am really, I'm just realising whilst writing this.

This next part is so surreal, not that everything so far hasn't been, but this was so unfathomable that I can't really begin to describe it, but I'll try. I heard a beeping sound, very low pitched, and some clicking coming from across the room. Then a large metal door slid open and, I couldn't believe my eyes, a tall, thin, dark greyish blue skinned creature walked into the room through the sliding door to my right. I was trying to digest what I was looking at, but the more I looked, the worse it got. This was a living nightmare on legs. I was beside myself with a cocktail of pain, anger, confusion, grief and terror and this creature walking in just made me chug it all.

I was startled by the thing, and it then looked over at me as I laid there whimpering. it's head was disproportionately larger than it's body, its face was symmetrical but had 6 black eyes that all blinked independently from one another, no nose but a gigantic mouth full of crooked, sharp, needle like teeth. It had only two fingers and a thumb, they were very long, thin and appeared to be slimy. It's skin had some darker blotches of blue on its hands and head, whilst it's spinal cord appeared to protrude from its back by at least 6 inches. It watched me squirm for a few moments before turning and approaching the table that Gary was on. It stopped at the side of the table, stared at the blood trail left behind for a moment and then picked up a strange contraption from below the table that looked a bit like a megaphone. It then used it to spray a substance onto the table, causing the blood to audibly fizz like a carbonated drink until it was essentially frozen, and it all shattered into dust, vanishing in the air and leaving the table spotless. I was stunned at what I was seeing and then the thing looked at me again with its six bulging eyes and raised a side of its mouth, displaying some of its gnarly teeth to me.

I laid back down, taking my eyes off of it and hoping to wake up from this like I did with the last bad dream but all I heard was its large feet scraping and slapping on the metallic floor below as it approached me. I looked up to see it standing over me. It had wrinkles exactly as a human would. Bags under its 6 eyes, crow's feet, jowls, excess skin. It was close enough for me to smell it. It smelled earthy, ironically, but sickly sweet too. It then extended a finger and touched my nose. My heart was pounding so fast, I felt nauseous and like I was about to pass out. It then shuffled to the side of my naked body and touched my belly button, all the while staring at me and emitting a light gurgling noise. But then it went lower and touched me in a place that only Alan is allowed to touch me, I think you understand what I'm saying, and I screamed at it. I also swung my arms at it, telling it to "get the fuck off me" and to never touch me again. This seemed to startle it as it stepped backwards and opened its toothy mouth. Then there was another buzzing sound that came from above, I don't know what this meant but it quickly scurried off back through the door it came from, and I laid there again, in tears, covering my mouth in sheer disbelief. I felt disgusted and violated and I needed to get out of this place. I then noticed it had left the megaphone like tool on the table next to me. I reached for it with all I had but couldn't quite reach it. So, I started spitting on my hands and rubbing it on my back and on my buttocks to lubricate myself. I was able to slide up about an inch before the metal belt holding me down clamped down around my hips. I yelped in pain, but once more tried to reach for the tool. By a mere fingertip's length, I was about to reach it.

I then pressed a button on the side of it and it whirred. I held it away from me and pressed down on the top as some liquid shot out of it in a perfect line and fizzed as it made contact with the table next to me. I then aimed it at the metal belt holding me down and shot at it. The belt fizzed and I heard a mechanical noise from underneath the slab I was on. Suddenly the belt came undone and popped off of me. I wasted no time, I jumped up in an instant and frantically searched for some clothes whilst

constantly looking over my shoulders and back at

the table I last saw Gary on, fighting back tears, but

I couldn't find any clothes at all. It was then that I

ran over to the other side of the room to look out

of the window. I was in an aircraft of some

description, hovering a few hundred feet from the

ground. It was pretty obvious to me, despite how

ludicrously ridiculous it sounded, that I was actually

in an alien spacecraft and had no idea how to

escape. But I walked to the door that the thing had

entered and exited through and saw Gary's shirt

and his underwear hanging on the wall. So, I took

them and quickly put them on, once I'd done that I

looked over and noticed a large button on the left side of the door, and without thinking I decided to press it and, to my surprise, it opened the door.

I didn't know what would be on the other side of the door, but I pressed the button, hoping it'd lead me to some kind of an exit. It opened with a screech and there was nothing but a dark hallway and an array of symmetrically placed flashing yellow lights on the blue walls and white ceilings. I had no idea what would happen to me if I was caught by one of those things, monsters, aliens, whatever you want to call them, so I searched for a weapon. Along the hallway I'd managed to find a sturdy pipe in a pile of random materials in a

corner. It appeared to be made of metal, but it was

unlike any material I'd ever held. It was black with

pink specks running through it like a gemstone but

felt like metal. I didn't take much time to consider

what it was, I just walked so very slowly around the

corner where I found another door, I was scared to

go in but also, I knew that if I didn't fight back, I'd

be dead anyway, so figured I might as well try.

I readied my pipe, took a deep breath and pressed

the button on the door. It slid open with a loud

crunch to reveal just another corridor with more

doors and strange symbols on the doors, the same

types of symbols engraved in the trees and on the walls of the corridors that I saw earlier. I didn't know what else to do other than press the button to open a door. So, I did and inside this room was a powerful green light that covered everything. Almost giving the same effect as ultraviolet but it was bright green. I could see the footsteps I was taking with my bare feet, they were leaving a trail behind me in the brighter hue of green but thankfully they vanished quickly.

As I got to the back of the room, I saw that there were rows of shelves all over this room with different sized containers lined up along them. I approached one of the shelves to see what was

being stored in the room and if it could help me in

anyway. I really wish I hadn't done that. Because I

saw that within these jars upon jars, they were full

of everything from fingers, toes, human noses,

nipples and even faces and penises. The shelf

behind it had organs from skin to hearts to lungs

and brains in jars and the ones behind that were

filled with bones. I covered my mouth in shock and

disgust and knew that I needed to get out of this

room but as I went to move, I heard a gargling noise

behind me.

I crouched down quickly to hide under a large

metallic desk like structure, keeping my hand over

my mouth to quieten my rapid breathing and

gripping my pipe so tightly that my knuckles turned

white. It was then that I heard the scraping and

slapping sounds again, just like I did when the thing

walked towards me in the room that I woke up in. I

looked down at the floor and felt a cold snap shoot

up my back when I saw my foot prints on the

ground leading to the desk I was hiding under. I

then felt my whole body go numb with fear as the

long, gangly legs of that thing walked past the desk.

Gargling more, like it had a mouthful of water. I

looked from under the desk and watched it's large,

bird like feet scratch the ground with its large talon

like claws and slop onto the floor with a thud. I

prayed that my footprints would vanish in time.

Then, just as it turned to approach the side of the

desk where my prints were, they vanished. I wanted

to sigh in relief but kept my hand firmly over my

mouth and nose. The thing stopped and stood by

the shelves I was just looking at, jingling one of the

jars, then it began walking back to the door, but

stopped right next to the desk I was under. I can

still smell the vomit inducing aroma of that room

and feel the level of fear I had when this thing was

stood mere inches from me. It was as if my eyes

were zooming in on its vibrant blue skin and dark

blue blotches, noticing all the veins in its muscles. It was unreal levels of terror. I imagined it was about to crouch down and catch me, so I readied my metal pipe but, to my surprise, it decided to just walk out. I didn't know if there were more of this thing or if it was alone or anything. But I did know I didn't want it to be anywhere near me. I waited a moment before getting out, but when I did, I noticed a new item on the shelf. It was a pectoral muscle, a man's chest in a large jar. I couldn't help but clutch my stomach and weep with agonising rage upon noticing a colourful, scratchy rose surrounded by the initials of my friends on the skin. I kissed my hand, touched the jar and said I was sorry before leaving. I loved him so much. I always will.

I left the room grief-stricken and stumbled into another door, pressing the button to enter without even thinking. But I snapped out of it suddenly as I walked into the room and felt a sudden drastic drop in temperature. It was incredibly cold in that room, so cold that frost began to form on my pipe within seconds. I looked around quickly, taking in the dirty green walls that were a sharp contrast from the white and blue covering most of the corridors and rooms. As I looked to the ceiling, I could see that there were icicles covering every square inch of it. I figured it was some sort of freezer but, in actuality, this room wasn't at all what I'd anticipated. I took a few steps inside as the large silver door closed behind me. I saw some large cylindrical gas or oil tanks to the right of me, I wasn't too sure what was in them; Still, I walked in 5 or so steps and despite the crippling chill of the frozen air surrounding me my skin began to crawl when I heard the gut-wrenching gargling noises again. Those noises caused my body to tense up and a chill to run down my spine that wasn't result of the freezer.

I crouched down, gripping my pipe tight and crept around the corner of one of the tanks. It was then that I dropped my pipe instantly, creating an almighty clang that reverberated around the large room, as I experienced absolute shock. I'd found Bruce and Dennis. My best friends. My brothers. Alan's Best Man and my Bridesmaid. Our family. But they were hanging naked and upside down. Gripped by their ankles that were trapped in a vice like mechanism that had snapped and bent their leg bones in all manner of unnatural contortions, twisting them around a circular loop with sharp shards of bone sticking out of their torn and over-stretched skin. Both had their backs to me until I approached them and saw something that was burned into my brain with such vibrancy that I will now see it whenever I close my eyes for the rest of my life. I could see as I approached them that both Bruce and Dennis had tubes in their throats sucking up blood into a smaller tank in front of them, I put my hand on Bruce's frozen and frostbitten skin as I turned to see their front sides. Dennis' face was half peeled off of his skull exposing his jaw, Bruce was missing his eyes, and both were missing their penis and testicles. I felt like I'd been shot in my stomach upon seeing that. I collapsed to the ground and screamed so hard that at first, I emitted no sound. It was a scream that was nothing but pure agony leaving my body. Gary, Bruce and Dennis were all gone with no way of getting them back and I still had no idea where Kit was. I told them through my tears that I loved them and that I was sorry, but then I heard the door open and the same scraping and slapping sounds bounced off the grotty walls of this frozen metal chamber. I quickly crouched and covered my mouth as I involuntarily screeched and crawled like a cowering animal to hide between two of the large cylindrical tanks.

The scraping and slapping noises were more akin to a stomp this time. I watched through the gap of the cylinders as the alien monster came into view. Gargling deeper this time like a growling rottweiler and it appeared to be much larger. It turned around suddenly, giving me a much greater view of its body

and I noticed it had a green stomach and green skin

under its chin, also it had 4 eyes instead of 6. I had

just learned in that moment that there were more

of them on the aircraft than the one I'd

encountered.

I stood still holding my breath as the thing stood in

place breathing heavily which made a rattling sound

in its throat not too dissimilar to a Rattlesnake

noise. It then slapped its long, stretched out lips

together which showed it's large, sharp teeth that

were more like knives than needles. Just as I

thought it was about to spot me, another buzzing

noise sounded off causing the thing to look upwards and instantly walk back out of the room. I could finally breathe again, I took a few moments to gain my composure and settle my heartrate before coming out from my hiding spot. I knew I had to get off the aircraft, but I still didn't know how. I was positive that I would die but wasn't about to lay down and let it happen easily, I owed it to Bruce, Dennis and Gary to tell their story and I'd hoped to find Kit somewhere aboard too. I got up, took a big breath, and approached my friends. I told them both how sorry I was and how I'd do anything to turn back time. After I said my final goodbyes to

Bruce and Dennis, I reluctantly left them behind and exited the frozen room.

I took another deep breath when the door closed behind me and continued down the corridor. When I reached the end, I turned the corner to see a large door slide open and out stomped the large 4 eyed being, this time it saw me. My eyes widened as it stood tall, puffing its chest out and showing its green tints on its chest and under its chin. Its mouth opened wide like a snake, and I could hear the clunking in its jaw as the bones or whatever it had for bones dislocated in order to widen its mouth further and displaying hundreds of dead straight, knife like teeth. The gargle turned into a roar that was almost identical to a tiger's and I took some steps backwards. That was when it erratically threw itself forward and began to chase me, flailing it's arms and legs around like they were independent from its body. I ran as fast as I could, glancing backwards and seeing this thing smashing and crashing into everything in its path and not even registering that it had done it. I turned a corner and came to the original door I'd left from, the door that led to the room I'd woken up in. I pressed the button to open it and ran inside whilst still hearing scrapes, shrieks and stomps of the creatures claws, throat and feet behind me. I turned to face the door and backed up towards a large metal console that was in the centre of the room. I accidentally leant against it and pressed a button that caused the hatch that opened and swallowed Gary's lifeless body to open once again, so I pressed it once more and it closed. I heard a snarling snap of teeth as the large bipedal scaley being walked into the room and began tilting its head and almost chirping at me with its throat puffing out like a bullfrog. Seeing it in such a clear light really did make it look quite reptile like to be honest, it was horrific. This one was taller than the last one, about 8 foot tall, its eyes were piercing and, despite them being fully black, I could tell they were fixed on me.

I asked what it wanted, and it just stared longingly

at me and walked slowly towards me, snarling and

drooling as thick saliva spilled from its mouth and

onto the floor looking like murky slop. I desperately

asked it to let me go, but it just stared at me blankly

with the deep, abyssal voids you'd call its eyes. I

was stammering as my entire body shook with

terror, I backed up around the table in a circle as

the thing followed me around it five or six times. I

was bawling and pleading for it to give me some

kind of information as to what it wanted and why it

was doing this to me, and why it killed my friends.

After experiencing total silence and overwhelming

intensity, I began to get angry and started swearing

at it. I called it so many names and even screamed

at it, showing my own teeth. As I did this, I stopped

walking and stood my ground, then I noticed that

when I'd stopped walking, it had also stopped and

was stood in place staring at me and breathing

heavily with a rattle in its throat. But what it hadn't

noticed was that it had stopped directly on the

chute that took Gary.

The idea sparked in my head instantly, I looked it

straight in the eyes and leapt forward, slamming my

open palm onto the button, causing the chute to

shoot open and the thing to have one of it's

muscular, yet bony legs fall inside, after that it

looked at me in a brand new way. Without

hesitation, I then whacked my hand down on the

button again to close the hatch on its leg. Which I

did. The thing screamed so loud that the room

vibrated, and the sounds bounced off of every

metallic surface. I covered my ears and watched as

a thick, blue liquid substance came seeping from its

leg and puddling around it as the chute door had

sliced all the way down to the bone. The screams

were even more deafening when it tried to violently

pull itself out, but instead it pulled and pushed so

hard that its leg separated from its body, and we

heard it drop into the chute. The being looked at

me and blinked multiple times, it then tried to

stand on its singular leg, but slipped on the puddle

of blue blood like liquid on the ground. It's screams

were getting quieter as it's blue blood was gushing

from its wound and it began to drag itself toward

me slowly, making croaky gurgling sounds, I

stomped on its three fingered hand and it barely

gave me a reaction but it continued to move

forward, I took some steps away as it slowed down

more and more. It turned onto it's back and I

watched as its chest and stomach, which were

soaked in its thick and sticky blood, begin to

vibrate. A large green tongue fell out of its mouth,

and I watched as it drew its final breath. It almost

froze in place when it exhaled. The darkness in its eyes somehow still had a light that dimmed as it died.

I collapsed to my knees upon seeing it die. I heard another buzzing sound above me, then after 10 seconds there was another buzz and another two more within 20 seconds. I stood up, fearing something was coming so I hid underneath the console that had the button on it.

Turns out I was right to do this as I heard another being enter the room and shriek upon seeing the body left behind. It ran over, stomping and wailing. I peered over the console to see the first blue creature I'd met cradling the being on the ground in its long, thin arms. I took my chance and crept to the edge of the table, then made a break for the door and ran down the corridor before hearing an ear-splitting scream coming from behind me. I ran and ran as fast as I could until I reached the room that the now dead creature walked out of before it chased me. I ran inside and pressed the button on the sliding door to close it behind me. The room was full of colourful buttons, shiny handles and bright lights. It had large windows around 80% of the room and a large, glowing circular platform in the centre of it. I couldn't read any of the writing on the buttons, but I knew this was the way off of the craft.

I was riddled with heavy set panic as I looked around the room and it was all alien to me. No pun intended. I stood still for a moment as the recent events played like a slideshow through my mind, wrenching my heart. My brain was in overdrive as I tried to wrap it around what had transpired. Which was when I heard the door to the room open and there, covered in the bright blue bodily fluids, stood the remaining alien. It's long, thin lips curled up revealing it's intimidating teeth as it snarled at me. It was so furious that it was frothing at the mouth and making a strange sound with every exhalation like it was in physical pain. "I had no choice" I said with a wobble and backing up into the room. I watched as it slowly but methodically scratched its long talons across the metal flooring with each long and drawn out step it took towards me. "You killed my friends" I told it as the saliva dripped from its frothing, trembling mouth. I backed away again and bumped into some sort of control panel. I screamed at it to back away but obviously it did no such thing. It was no more than 3 feet from me when I decided I had to make a run for it. As I attempted to break away, I quickly ducked under its side and ran towards the door but it's long arms stretched out with a creak and it's cold, clammy hand snatched me up off my feet. I can still feel the thing's three

fingered hand digging it's fingertips into my throat.

It raised me up off the ground and moved around, I

grabbed it's moist and cold wrist as it screamed a

deathly howl in my face. I felt it's breath collide

with my eyes and creep up my nostrils, it was

odourless but warm and I saw that it's tongue and

throat were bright yellow. I was beyond petrified,

thinking those jaws and yellow throat were how I

was about to die, so I readied myself for a horrific

and a painful death.

Still elevated off the ground by my throat, I was

praying I would die from asphyxia before it did

anything to me. The creature then looked at me with its mouth open baring its crooked needle teeth and its 6 deep black eyes blinking just slightly out of time with each other, it then lowered its lips and relaxed it's breathing, then, just before I passed, it just dropped me and walked away from me. Shaken, tense and gasping for air, I asked it what it was doing, despite knowing I'd get no response. I winced as it took a step towards me once more and pointed at me. I didn't understand so I asked again for any kind of answer. But all I got was a final glimpse at the being before looking down and realising I was on top of the glowing platform in the centre of the room. The floor opened, my heart stopped, and I expected to come hurtling hundreds

of feet to the ground to my death. But I didn't.

Instead, I was steadily lowered in a bright blue

beam, safely to the ground, right next to Dennis'

car. I was in a state of true horror. I was crying tears

of mourning, stress, sadness and joy all at the same

time. I was a hysterical mess to say the least.

My bare feet finally touched the ground. The grass

on my skin felt orgasmic after what I'd just

experienced. So, I stood firm on my feet, looking at

the red sky as dawn broke over the horizon, I was

dressed in nothing but Gary's dirty white t-shirt that

was 4 sizes too big on me and had a pink skull on it

and his rainbow coloured underwear to boot. I wept hard as a plethora of emotions washed over me like a tsunami. I sharply looked around me expecting to see a circle of hooded figures, but thankfully I saw no one else there. No one screaming, chanting or jeering at me. No creepy culty bastards; just me. The beam of light then suddenly recoiled back into the sky like a blue glass tube, I saw no alien craft in the sky only the light vanish into nothingness. I felt unfathomably scared but also very relieved in that moment. That might sound selfish after what happened, in fact, I know it does to some, but that relief was soon shattered as separate beams shone down onto the camp site. I had no clue what to expect. Was it about to take

me again? Was it about to shoot me? Was the thing

coming off the ship? None of those were correct.

Actually, what happened was, I saw 3 dark objects

descending inside the beams and squinted my eyes

in an attempt to see what they were. I couldn't

make it out. But as they landed softly, equally

spaced out around me I rushed over to get a better

look and saw Gary, Bruce and Dennis' mutilated

corpses laying on the wet grass next to the tent.

Seeing them in the ship was one thing, but now

back on the ground was inexplicably horrendous.

Their blood everywhere, their organs missing, skin

peeled. It is beyond words and all I could do was

drop to my knees and let out a sorrowful scream into the sky. The beams then suddenly shone blindingly bright and, in a fraction of a second, silently shot up into the sky and vanished out of sight. I sat, traumatised, next to my boys in total shock. I hugged their lifeless bodies, telling them how sorry I was over and over. The sun had almost fully arisen when a bright blue flashing light shone over me and the guys, I braced myself to be taken again, I closed my eyes and expected the beam to hit me when I heard a deep voice shout "Hands in the air. Do not move, Ma'am!" I turned with a jolt to see 4 Police Officers standing with their firearms pointed directly at me. I tried to speak but before I could get any words out, I was taken to the ground

by two officers who told me "Miss, you are under

arrest." I went numb and couldn't believe what I

was hearing, I started to protest and tell them it

wasn't me, but they then read me my Miranda

rights and brought me to my feet. I saw I was now

covered in my best friends' blood. The police asked

if I understood my rights and I just nodded and

went with them, staring at Bruce, Gary and Dennis

as I was led away to the police car. I was placed in

handcuffs, in a daze, and I overheard one of the

officers mention how the report came in from an

older man who was out hunting with his dog when

he discovered a body in the woods. I wanted to

hear more but I was then shoved into the back of the cruiser and taken to the local police station.

I was interrogated for 14 hours over the course of 2 days. I told them everything that happened as I've just written it here, but they didn't believe me. Obviously. How could anyone believe that? They asked me why I killed them, and I told them I didn't. They asked me how I did it, when, why Kit was so far from the others, what I did with their penises, etc. and I told them I didn't do anything at all. I stuck to the truth, but it was falling on deaf ears. They showed me the autopsy pictures of all of my friends, which caused me to vomit into the trash can in the room. They then showed me Kit's body.

He'd been stabbed 66 times all over his body, his

eyes had been removed, his tongue was cut out and

his throat had been cut so deeply he was almost

decapitated. I couldn't stomach that either. I was an

emotionally drained mess and was hardly even

coherent as the interrogation drew to a close. The

officers finished their interview, and I went back to

my cell with nothing but my mind, my torturous

memories and the vacant walls for company. It was

the 3rd day when Alan was able to visit me. I was so

excited to see him and felt desperate for a hug and

for him to kiss my head and tell me everything will

be okay and that everyone was in my corner. He

walked in the door, my heart was racing, it was the first time I'd seen him in almost 5 days. I sprung up from my chair to hug him, but as soon as he saw me, he turned his face away and walked to the other side of the table I was sat at. I felt a strange tensions in the air; one I hadn't anticipated. I stared at him with my bloodshot eyes and said "what's going on, babe?" to which he looked at me tearfully and said with a hoarse voice "I've been asking myself the same damn thing for the last 3 days, Tammy." I sat down on my creaky plastic chair as he sat on his in silence, staring at his quivering clenched fists. He looked up and asked me "why did you do those things to our best friends, Tam? They were your brothers! They loved you so deeply." I began to tremble as I realised that he too believed I was capable of this. I started to say that I didn't do anything, but he viciously cut me off by slamming his hand on the table. He stared at me as if he was staring through me and barked "they're saying you're talking about aliens abducting you and doing all of this to Bruce and the boys. Have you lost your fucking mind, Tammy? You sound like a basket case!" I asked him how he thinks I could do these things to the boys, why would I say it was an abduction if it wasn't true? But he placed his hands over his face and told me that those questions weren't for him to answer and said that just because there are some "bullshit spooky stories" surrounding Blue Rock doesn't mean I will get away with murdering 4 innocent men. He stood up and said "Look, I cannot do this. My heart is shattered. I can't. I want to believe you, you have no idea how badly, but I just can't. I know you did this, Tammy. I don't know why, but I know you did. So, we are done." He stood up and began to walk towards the door, I sat in disbelief, feeling my stomach tie itself in a knot and the hairs raise on my arm as my future was heading towards the exit. But he paused for a moment and I had fleeting hope that he was having second thoughts, he looked up at me with teary glint in his eye and said "You can keep the ring."

before opening the door and walking out, slamming the door behind him, I heard him crying deeply, practically wailing outside the door the second it shut. I sat inside, staring at the blank wall as tears streamed down my face and splashed on the table top. I was beyond heartbroken. I felt trapped and like I just needed to die. "I should have just let them take me too." I said aloud to myself. I spent the next 8 months in a psychiatric hospital on suicide watch after attempting to take my own life multiple times. I was being treated for anything and everything in hopes that it would help get to the bottom of what was happening. Paranoid delusions, psychopathy, psychosis and schizophrenia were all brought up, because people would rather hide their

heads in the sand before acknowledging the truth.

When my court date finally came, my lawyer tried

so hard and told the story exactly as it happened. I

had character statements from people who'd

known me my whole life, my parents testified in my

defence, and we even had witnesses come forward

to say they'd seen strange lights in the sky that very

night over Blue Rock. But still, it took the jury less

than 5 minutes to decide that I was guilty of

murdering my best friends. The prosecution

claimed that I had sent the texts that I'd received

from Gary on my phone after murdering my friends

in an attempt to cover my tracks with "ludicrously

dramatic fiction", they then said I'd destroyed the phones and thrown them into a lake or buried them nearby in order to conceal anything that would prove my story false. There was no sign of a voicemail message from Gary either as the phones were never recovered. Despite me hearing it with my own ears, it wasn't used as evidence in my defence as they couldn't verify it was really there. The cell phone company was contacted, and they did verify that there were phone calls made to my number and they confirmed a call being connected, however they couldn't verify a voicemail being left. Which didn't make sense because there truly was one. They also brought in the old man who'd found

Kit's body. His name was Oliver and was the same old man we'd all met in the woods earlier in the day. He was called as a witness in court and said that I'd seemed disconnected and distracted when he'd met us. He said that I made him feel uneasy with my "unhealthy fascination" with the cult activity at Blue Rock. Which I can't confirm to be false, but I highly suspect it was. The final nail though, came from the small metal candle burner I'd taken as a souvenir. It was said to be linked to other disappearances and cult activity, since my defence for having it in my possession was "I found it in the woods" I was pretty screwed. So, after many sessions in court, I was eventually sentenced to serve 4 consecutive life sentences for murder in the 1st degree, which accumulated to 96 years in prison. Which is where I am right now as I write this to you, Dr Johnstone.

I've been here for the last 18 months nearly, and I've lost everything besides my mom and dad. My friends, extended family, Alan's side of the family, they've all disowned me and turned their backs on me and how could anyone blame them? My Mom told me that Alan has moved on and is with another woman now, that shattered my heart but ultimately, I want him to be happy. I get mail from the guys' families and friends sometimes telling me to "burn in hell" or "hurry up and die" too. I'm trying to appeal my sentence, but I don't know how that'll go. Well, I do know really. I'll never get out of here, but I don't deserve to be in here at all. The press only covered the shocking bits and chopped their quotes to suit their own narrative to sell papers and get clicks on their website. I'm hoping that by writing this, someone else who has experienced these beings or has some sort of proof could help me. It's a long shot, sure. But it's all I've got.

Thank you for taking the time to read this. I hope this makes it into your book.

Regards,

Tammy

Doctor's Notes – This story not only intrigued me, but also baffles and sickens me. I'm aware this is a sensitive subject for those of whom are personally connected to this case, and I deeply apologise if my publishing this has caused you harm in any way. But I couldn't ignore it.

Of course, this is a story that is very difficult to wrap your mind around. Cults, mind bending group hysteria, alien abduction and the tragic loss of some wonderful men. I read this story over and over trying to make sense of it. I, of course, have heard of Blue Rock National Park and the bizarre goings on that are alleged to have been witnessed there. But never would I ever have anticipated something on this scale.

I made the decision to visit Tammy in Saundersville Prison. When I saw her walking towards me in chains and cuffs I was stunned. This 5 foot nothing 100lb girl did not look like someone capable of doing something of the likes she is accused of. I spoke with Tammy about what happened and seeing her tell me in person, rather than just reading it on paper, was truly eye-opening. I apologise to anyone this may offend, but I believe her.

The creatures that Tammy encountered were not of this earth, but also don't fit the description of any other *'alien' type being I've ever heard of. Not Grey's,*

Reptilians, Space Brothers, Vertikrans or Islyopicans.

There's just not enough research or even any basic

information on these beings for me to even suggest

anything about them. The cult, however, I have heard

of. They call themselves 'The Children of the Chosen'.

This cult has operated for upwards of 150 years in Blue

Rock and are scattered all over the USA and potentially

even worldwide. They are very secretive and elusive, but

I have a source who tells me that these 'Children' are

people who rank high and low in society. Some are

librarians, waiters, teachers and customer service

agents and others are police, judges, politicians and

lawyers. Whoever they are, they're dangerous and very

well hidden in plain sight. No one knows who these

'Children of the Chosen' are. Maybe they're your child's teacher, your local shop worker, maybe even your neighbour. – HJ

Story IV – The Gifts

The year was 1995, I had just turned 17 and was sat on my bed reading the latest comic from my favourite comic book series, The Great Valkat. She is a warrior space Queen who always fights for her people and kicks everybody's ass. I idolised her. I'd been waiting a month for this issue to release and just as I was sinking my teeth into the story, I heard the front door open.

My Dad had come home from another one of his

overnight work trips away, I knew it was Dad

because his keys had about a thousand keyrings on

them that always made the same jingling sounds.

He called up the stairs to me, "Hillary? Hillary are

you home?". I let out a loud groan as I knew I had

to put my comic on pause. "Yeah, Dad." I said with a

run of the mill teenage grunt. He'd walked through

to the living room but I could faintly hear him call

"Can you come down here please?", which I ignored

so I could continue my comic but he came back and

asked again, this time from the bottom of the stairs,

so I had no choice but to answer him this time.

"Yes. Fine." I said, passive aggressively slamming

down my comic on my duvet.

As I got to the top of the stairs, I could hear the rustling of some bags. "Dad has gone shopping on his way home & just wants me to put it all away like usual" I thought to myself as I descended the stairs. But when I got around the doorframe into the living room, I turned to look into the kitchen & saw my dad hunched over, his bald head greeting me as he unpacked the shopping on the counter next to his work tools. He looked up at me with his big goofy grin peeking out of his bushy greying beard and said "Ah, it's a miracle! It's alive!" A joke he makes approximately 3 times a week. I gave him the usual response of a middle finger & he did his usual

response of telling me to "watch my language."

To that I said "I'm using sign language, watching is

kind of the point.". He smiled again and closed his

eyes in sarcastic acknowledgment.

I swept my jet black hair over my ears, then put my

hands in the front pocket of my hoodie and said "do

you actually need me for anything or can I go back

up and read my.." but he sharply cut me off with

excited glee and said "I went to a second hand shop

today and found something I think you'll like!", I

was surprised as usually it was Mum that would buy

the random presents, but I guess since she was

gone now he was trying to fill that gap. He couldn't, no one ever could. But I was always grateful when he tried.

"What is it?" I said as if I didn't care but really, I did, because underneath my 'Goth' exterior, with my dark hair, dark makeup & jet black clothes still lived that little girl who loved when her Dad bought her things. "Well, I was walking around the store to find some new books to read, but I saw this on a shelf and had to get it for you" he said excitedly, then he reached into one of his bags, rustling around like a fox in a bin, and pulled out this dusty old ceramic cat ornament.

He presented it to me like it was the holy grail or something. "A cat? Why?" I asked with a squint, Dad's face dropped and said "I thought you'd love it. You're always talking about that super cat you read about!" I sighed and said "No, Dad. That's Volkat. She is a warrior Queen from the planet Darriads 2711. Not some dusty old tabby cat with a cracked face."

Dad looked down at his feet, put his hands in his pockets, took a sharp breath in and said "I'm sorry, sweetheart." Then looked up at me and said "I guess I need to pay more attention, huh?". In my head I thought "Less attention actually. That would be perfect. Thanks!" But out loud what I actually said was "I actually love it. It's pretty cute when you stare at its fucked up little face long enough". Dad's face broke out in a grin & he pointed at me with a smiley side stare. "I know I know. 'Language'." I said as I turned to go back upstairs with my new fragile feline friend.

When I got to my room, I looked for the perfect spot to display my new gift in all it's cracked face glory.

I figured on my comic bookcase would be most fitting, since he was meant to be the "super cat" I always talk about. I found a great spot on the top shelf and I placed it facing my window, lining it up

perfectly so as to stand guard and be the watchful

eye that a super cat would be; I stood for a moment

and watched the snow fall from the sky, I

remember it all looking so tranquil but feeling

nothing but dread. Just as soon as I'd recognised my

anxiety, I'd remembered I hadn't said thank you to

Dad for this gift, so I quickly turned and ran

downstairs.

I got down and Dad was still unpacking his work

tools and his shopping, which was mostly food,

sauces, seasonings, etc. Dad liked to cook. Without

any words I just swung my arms around him and

gave him the biggest hug. He almost felt like he was shaking, I'm not the most affectionate person and especially not since my Mum died 10 months ago. but this hug was one I'll never forget. He slowly wrapped his arms around my shoulders and rested his bearded face on the top of my head. "Thank you" I whispered. His chest bounced off my face as he gave a small chuckle and said "No, kiddo. Thank you. Without you I don't even know what I would do.". I looked up at him and saw the tears filling his eyes as he smiled at me and so I wiped the tears from his eyes, called him a loser, as I often affectionately did, and hugged him even tighter. The shaking stopped, he kissed the top of my head and said my 4 favourite words in the English language;

"Do you want food?". To which my answer is always a resounding "Yes!".

Dad always made a huge dinner after his work trips. He would always do a huge shopping trip on the way home and make a feast fit for a Royal Family, every time bringing home these big cuts of meat wrapped in paper, huge leaves of herbs and bottles of spices, sacks of vegetables all that I assumed he'd gotten from a Butcher somewhere on his journey back.

I stayed downstairs talking with Dad for hours.

Laughing and joking as he cooked us up a 5 star meal, just like we always used to do. We hadn't done that for a while.

When the final morsel of food had been consumed and the last drop of fizzy pop had been drunk, I said goodnight to Dad and headed to my room to finally read my Comic in bed until I fell asleep.

When I woke up in the morning to my dad mowing the lawn, I realised I'd fallen asleep with my comic in my hands. So, I quickly got up, threw on some clothes and went to put my comic on my bookcase when I noticed that my new 'Super Cat' ornament was not where I had left it.

I looked on the other shelves, the floor around the bookcase, I looked behind it and even under my bed, but I couldn't see it anywhere. I figured maybe Dad had moved it, but he never comes into my room when I'm sleeping. I thought it was weird but figured there was a reason, like maybe Dad wanted to fix its face & surprise me or something. I walked out of my bedroom, closing the door behind me. I walked down our dimly lit hallway to the stairs and noticed on my dad's bedside table that my little Cat buddy was sitting there. So, I picked it up and took it downstairs with me.

I went into the kitchen and left it on the counter as I

got myself my usual glass of OJ and a bowl of cornflakes when my dad walked in from outside the back garden. "Oh, did the lawn mower wake you?" He said in an apologetic tone. "Yeah, that thing is so loud!" I said with a smile. Dad met my smile with one of his own and said "Sorry Kiddo, I should've known it was too loud" then his eyes quickly shifted to the ornament on the counter and reach over, as he was picking it up he said "how come you brought this to me last night?". I didn't quite know what he meant so I just tilted my head and made a "eh?" sound, raising the corner of my lip.

Dad laughed and said "Ah, I knew it. I knew you were sleepwalking." I raised my eyebrows in shock, "sleepwalking!?" I said with a sudden jolt of

disbelief.

"Yeah, you used to do it sometimes as a kid." Dad

said but paused himself for a moment and

continued "Well, as a littler kid anyway. Usually

before going back to school after a holiday or

something."

I laughed and said I couldn't have because my

Comic was still in my hands when I woke up, but he

was insistent that I did, and that I'd brought it to

him.

"Well, I guess I'll just take it back then." I said with a

mildly nervous chuckle. Dad stared at me with his

dad face, and I knew he was going to say something Dad-like. "You know, Hil. You can always talk to me about what you're feeling. Even if you think you can't, you can. Chances are, I'm feeling it too. It's been a rough year for us. Your Mum talking her own life was.." he paused for a moment, shook his head and continued "Look, what I'm saying is that I didn't expect it, but I'm not too surprised you're sleepwalking again." He said with his eyes on me, I could feel them burning into my soul as I tried to avoid them at all costs. "I know Dad. Thanks" I said sharply as an attempt to stop the Fatherly concern, as I said, I've never been one to be that affectionate, but also, I don't like talking about my feelings. I prefer to pretend everything's okay by ignoring the shitty feelings, bottle it all up until it becomes unbearable, have a mini breakdown and then start the process all over again.

"Okay then, kid." He said with a single nod. "I better get back out and finish this lawn before it rains. It looks like a storm's brewing." He said leaning back with his thumb pointing to the garden as he quickly went out of the sliding door.

I looked over at the ornament and speedily picked it up to look at it, I studied it's chipped face and then looked on the bottom of it. I found a price sticker that I peeled off; the sticker left a sort of gunky residue like the sticker had been there for a long time, but underneath the gunk I could make out a small logo. I assume for the people who made the thing. I could just about make out the word "village", but I didn't care enough to dirty my nails picking off the residue to reveal the top part of the name.

I went back upstairs after breakfast and placed the Cat back on the shelf it was living on before. In exactly the same place.

Later in the evening, it was almost time for bed, I went downstairs to say goodnight to Dad, but I couldn't find him. I called his name a bunch of times, even using his real name, "Matt", I called but got no response. I thought it was strange, so I went to check the garden and saw him standing in the middle of the yard, with no shoes, socks or jacket, just staring at the stars.

I went outside, wrapping my jacket around myself as the cold air hit my body, "Dad?" I said quietly but he didn't respond to me again. I walked up and put my hand on his shoulder, "Dad, what are you doing?" I said through my chattering teeth. He turned to me with his eyes full of tears and just about squeaked out "I just miss her so much." as he lowered his head and began to sob. I didn't know what to do or say, because I know that nothing I do or say could take this pain away. I knew that all too well. I just rubbed his back and brought him back inside to the kitchen counter where we sat in silence for a few moments. When he caught his breath, he apologised and said he needed to be "strong" for me, to which I told him that macho crap was unnecessary with me. "I know this hurts you just as much as it hurts me, Dad. I miss her too." I paused for a moment as I took 3 sharp breaths to hold the tears back, "every moment of every day" I said as the tears rolled down my face. "Life feels empty without her." I said as I felt Dad's hand gently wipe the tears from my face. I looked up at him and he had that goofy smile on his face again as he said "Who's the loser now?", which actually made me laugh out loud and we hugged so tightly for what felt like half an hour after that.

After we said our goodnights, I went to bed and shut off my light to go to sleep.

I felt peaceful as I drifted off and then almost instantly I was being shaken awake hearing "Hillary! Hillary, sweetheart! Wake up! Wake up!" It was my dad's voice and he sounded panicked. I remember becoming conscious of where I was, I was in my dad's room and he was sat on his bed with his arms on my shoulders, staring into my eyes as they cracked open, I looked at him and frowned. "What's going on?" I drowsily uttered. I glanced down as I noticed my hands were clenched shut, almost like they were cramping and there was blood all over my hand, dripping down in a thick pool of crimson on my dad's cream coloured bedroom carpet. As I noticed this my hands almost instantly released their tension. As they relaxed, the cat ornament fell from grip and into the puddle below. Spattering a droplet or two of blood onto our bare feet. I had a deep cut on my thumb where I'd been gripping the ornament and pressing my thumb into its broken face. I looked up at my dad and he just looked horrified, like he'd seen a ghost or something. Not that I could blame him.

He took me downstairs to the kitchen to get the wound washed and bandaged up, I took note of the time on the wall clock, 3:38am, I was still so tired but the pain in my thumb kept me up. As Dad was bandaging my hand, he looked at me and said "maybe we need to throw that ornament out now?", but as much as I mocked him for it in the beginning, it really meant a lot to me, so I said I didn't want to. He explained that it may be a trigger, because twice in 2 days I'd brought it to his room whilst sleepwalking and I'd injured myself on it. He had a point, a very good point, but I didn't want to lose something that the only parent I have

left had bought me. So, I said I'd find a new place to

display it, not so close to my bedroom door. He told

me it would make him more comfortable if we

threw it out, but he wanted me to make the choice

myself. I decided to keep it, so I washed it off & put

it on the other side of my room, in an empty plastic

collectible figure case that had no collectable figure

in it.

I went to say goodnight to Dad again, I found him

on his hands and knees scrubbing his bedroom floor

with bleach, trying to clean my blood off. I felt

guilty and asked if he needed any help, but Dad said

"the best help you can give me right now is going and getting some decent sleep. I love you, Honey. Goodnight". So, I did just that.

I was taken to see our doctor the next day and dad made sure he was with me. Seemed he was very worried about me and wanted to make sure there was nothing more serious than sleep walking going on with me. According to Doctor Baron, it was all very normal, and they said I was very stressed what with my Mum's passing and finishing school. So, they advised me to do a few things differently. Like go to bed at the same time every night, read a book before bed and make sure my room was quiet, which I did already so I thought it was all totally useless information.

On the way home from the Doctor's, Dad and I went to a home supplies shop in town, and he ended up buying a stair gate for the top of the stairs, the same one used to toddlers. In fact, I remember that it had a toddler on the box too. I was mortified. I begged him not to do it, I said he was overreacting, but he did it anyway. He said "you could fall and break your neck", which now I see as a sensible choice. But as a 17 year old girl with a rebellious reputation to uphold I was not happy about it.

But a week had soon passed since then with no new

sleepwalking episodes being reported to me.

Everything felt kind of normal again, except I was

starting to feel really under the weather. My nose

was running, and I had a constant headache, but I

did my best to ignore it and just powered through

as I normally did. My Dad had told me a few days

before that he had to go out to a job 300 miles

away today and would be gone overnight. I was

okay with that, I always loved having the house to

myself. Whereas Dad on the other hand was riddled

with worry because of my sleepwalking antics. But

he said we need the money, so I told him not to

worry. I'd not had an episode in a week so I told him to go ahead with the job, assuring him I would be fine.

Dad was looking at a map, making sure he knew where to go and how to get there, then he looked up, clicked his fingers and weirdly asked if he could take my cat statue with him. He said it would make him feel better if he had it with him just in case it triggered another sleepwalking episode. I laughed, I thought it was weird, but I shrugged and said "Well, I guess. So long as you bring it back.". He did a dramatic sigh of relief, thanked me and promised to keep it safe in a really sarcastic tone. I didn't understand why he was being a prick. I figured he was just stressed about the job and his worrying and stuff. But I didn't like it.

I went upstairs quickly and got it for him, and then I watched him put it in his bag, handling it like a bomb, pretending like it was a rare antique or something. I knew he was joking with me because I asked him to be careful with it but, for some odd reason, this coupled with his awkward joke from before had made me really angry. So, I sharply told him to have a nice trip and just went upstairs to my room.

20 minutes pass and Dad comes upstairs, goes to

his room to get a few extra things, I can hear a

shuffle of some papers and a briefcase clipping

shut, every sound he made just irritated me more.

He peered into my room and said "I'm going now,

Hil. I'll be back tomorrow. I've left the numbers for

where I'm gonna be staying and where I'm working

next to the phone. Call if you need anything. Love

you.".

I still felt incredibly mad at him, and my headache

was severe, so I just replied with "Goodbye. Be

safe.". He came in and sat with me for a moment,

put his big burley hand on my arm and told me that

he loved me. I didn't say it back. I was still too mad.

But as he was leaving the house, he said it again

and I actually went to shout it back to him, but I was too tired. I felt my consciousness slip away and I fell into a deep sleep. I woke up with a startling gasp in what seemed like two seconds, but I knew it had been a lot longer because it was dark now and the moon was shining through the windows leaving shadows of the window frames on the floor. I sat up and rubbed my face, but when I stood up, I felt heavy and like I was walking through waist deep water. I wondered why I felt so unwell when I'd just had a nap. I walked over to my light and switched it on, but the bulb didn't turn on, I figured the bulb had blown. A nuisance, but no big deal. We had bulbs in the cupboard under the stairs.

I could see it was raining outside from the shadows of the dripping drops on the windows. From the way the moon hit them, it was as if I was watching the silhouettes of slithering snakes going across my floor. I then heard a gigantic gust of wind rattle my window and it frightened me. So, I darted out of my room and quickly turned the hallway light switch on to give me some light, but again, no light came.

"Damn! I think the power might be out" I thought to myself. I went back into my room to get some tealight candles and a lighter from my drawer. I began placing lit candles wherever I could as I was making my way downstairs, through the living room and to the kitchen to find a torch. When I got into

our Kitchen it was so cold that I could see my own

breath in moonlight shining through the sliding

doors. I scrabbled in the crap drawer to find the

torch, you know the crap drawer? Everyone has one

in their house. Where you put the random stuff like

notebooks, tape, string, random wall fixings and

stuff. That's where I found our torch. I turned it on,

shone it straight across the kitchen, into the living

room and froze solid with bone-chilling shock when

I saw the legs of a person standing in the dark just

out of the torches beam trajectory.

I moved the torch light over towards the legs, trying

to control the shaking from both the cold and the sight of seeing a strange person in my home, lurking in the dark. Their legs were cut and bleeding, but they stood totally still. Just as I got enough courage to shine the light on their face, the torch flickered on and off for a second, I hit it frantically to get it to turn back on and when it did the person had vanished.

I was terrified, cold and in the dark. With a stranger in my house. During a power outage. Safe to assume I was absolutely freaking out. I couldn't even call my dad because this was 1995 and we only had a landline phone, which was knocked out in the power cut. So, I did all I could in the moment.

I grabbed a big knife from the knife block and

slumped in the corner of the kitchen.

I could hear things shuffling around, in the living

room, I could see things being thrown around in the

flickers of the flames atop the tealights. I was

scared and trying to wrap my 17 year old head

around the reality of potentially having to stab

someone if they got too close. But then it suddenly

all went quiet. So quiet I could only hear the rain on

the glass sliding doors. Hammering down against it

in the heavy winter winds. I stood up, shakily

holding my knife in one hand and my flickering

torch in the other. My fingers were numb and stinging from the cold, but I stood there still as a statue, watching.

I was going to ask who was there, but just as I began to speak, the furthest candle away from me went out and it startled me. Then the next one closest to it went out and I started to get really anxious. But then, as if they were running out of time exactly one second after the other, every candle went out one by one in a row coming towards me until only one candle remained burning. The one closest to me on the kitchen counter. My flashlight finally died right there and then as if it had seen all this unfold and gotten scared to death.

I was so scared of what was happening that I decided to close my eyes tight and grip the knife even tighter. But then I heard someone blow the candle out right in front of me.

I could hear breathing. Deep, raspy breathing. I heard what sounded like wet, bare feet slapping on the kitchen floor coming toward me. I could feel their breath on my face, I didn't dare open my eyes. I felt their cold, bony fingers on my temple as they slowly slid down and squeezed my jaw.

Keeping my eyes firmly closed, I heard a clicking

sound, like the sound you'd hear if you stuck your tongue to the roof of your mouth and pulled it away quickly. Like 6 or 7 clicks really fast. I was petrified. But then I imagined what Volkat would do and asked myself if she would be scared. I decided swiftly that she might be a little scared, but she would always defend her home against intruders. So, I readied myself with the knife and opened my eyes to strike; but whoever was there, was suddenly gone. So, naturally, I ran for the front door to escape. My immediate plan was to run to the police station, despite having nothing on my feet, but I didn't even make it to the door. I got to the bottom of the stairs before every photograph we had on the wall going up the stairs came hurtling down the stairs, sending broken glass and picture frame debris all over the hallway to the front door. I fell back into the living room after seeing this.

I crawled deeper into the dark living room, its only light from the moon that is now almost fully covered in clouds. I hid behind the couch peering just barely over the top of it, on lookout for whoever was invading my house and smashing up my pictures.

I heard a footstep on the stairs. Loud and heavy. Then I heard another follow slowly after it. They were bold and thunderous steps that echoed throughout the house. I waited behind an armchair and hid underneath a thin blanket counting each step I heard. After 16 steps, I heard them come to a halt. The next step was slow and crunchy, so I knew they were downstairs walking across the broken glass and wood on the floor. I decided to peak over my couch but just as I went to, I heard that familiar clicking noise and hid again.

After a few moments of trembling, listening to the shuffling and the clicking, I just felt this sudden burst of anger and confidence brew within me. I jumped up, with a buzzing feeling in my head and over my body and said "Hey! Whoever you are, get the fuck out of my house now!" The room fell silent,

growing noticeably colder and darker. I said it again

but a lot shakier "get out of my house! I have a

knife!" just as I finished saying the last word at the

top of my lungs and hearing nothing in response, I

felt strangely relaxed and proud of myself. Until I

looked up at the mirror directly across from me on

the living room wall.

Stood next to me in my reflection was a naked

woman covered in blood, battered and bruised,

missing an eye and had a dislocated jaw so severe

that the only sound she was able to make was that

same clicking noise I'd been hearing. I collapsed on

the ground, dropping the knife on the ground. I

thought I was going insane. "Did I just see a ghost?"

I thought. "Am I dreaming?" I screamed out as I was

pinching and slapping myself to wake up, but I was

still there on the living room floor. She wasn't there

when I looked beside me, she had vanished.

Panicking, I asked myself "What am I supposed to

do?" but just as my head began to race with ideas, I

heard a knock coming from upstairs. My instinct

told me to follow it, but my brain instantly halted

me to ask if I was crazy. After a short deliberation,

my instinct won. I hurriedly went to the stairs and

hopped over the shattered remains of the pictures

on the floor.

As I went upstairs, I noticed that some pictures were still on the wall. My pictures. I was confused and afraid but when I heard the knock again, I went and followed it straight upstairs.

Upon reaching the top of the stairs I saw that dad's bedroom door was open now, but it was closed before I came downstairs. I wondered how that happened but as I did, I heard the knock again coming from inside the room. I was shaken but had a gut feeling that I needed to follow this knocking sound. When I got inside his room, it was dark and quiet. I took one step in and shakily whispered "hello?", just as the final syllable left my lips, I could hear the slow, striking strum of knuckles on wood again over by his bed. Disturbed, yet determined, I leapt across his floor and looked all over the space. The ceiling, the wall, under the bed, but I saw nothing and no one. I was convinced I was half asleep and perhaps having a fever dream from this sickness I had come down with, after all I didn't exactly know how this whole sleepwalking thing worked. But just as I sighed some relief at the prospect of it all being in my head, I suddenly felt overwhelmingly weary and scared beyond comprehension. I observed the clouds move as the moon shone inside the darkened room I was sat in.

The moon lit up and shone on the space next to Dad's bed. Then I heard the knocking again, coming from under the floor by his bed. I told myself "That could be anything though. Next door closing doors, or the wind blowing against the house or something" so I got down on my hands and knees and put my ear to the floor to make sure I was correct, and I wasn't losing my mind. But it knocked again, so hard that I felt it on my cheek, and I jumped up feeling all the blood rush from my face. So now I knew this was real and not in my head. I needed to know what was under there. Was there a person stuck there? Did they need my help? I was overcome with ascertainment.

I picked up and moved his bedside table to the side, which uncovered a convenient slice in the carpet so that I could lift it up, like a little flap. The table was on it, presumably to keep it weighed down. I peeled it back but found nothing but old, cracking floorboards. However, one thing I noticed more than anything else, was how shiny some of the screws were in the moonlight, but bizarrely it was just one of the floorboards that was screwed in with these shiny screws. Like they had only recently been screwed in.

So, I decided to go downstairs and get a screwdriver from the shed outside. As I got up to my feet to go downstairs, I walked past the mirror hanging over my dad's bed and saw 4 more figures standing behind me out of the corner of my eye. I turned to look directly at them, but they weren't there. However, if I turned my head, I could still see them in my peripheral vision. All women. They too were roughed up and bleeding. I could hardly breathe through the fear but then I hear what sounds like 40 hands violently knocking on the floor, it was overpoweringly loud. So as the goosebumps ran all over my body I too ran downstairs to the kitchen, jumping over the glass in the hallway as I went. I grabbed the key and ran out of the door to the shed.

I quickly unlocked the shed and found the tools easy enough, but as I walked out, I could see the figures of at least 10 women in all the upstairs windows of the house. Illuminated by the lunar beams emanating from the sky.

I thought to myself that only a fool would go in the house after seeing this, but somehow, I still felt compelled to do it.

I went back inside and straight upstairs, avoiding all the mirrors as I did. I got to my dad's room, rolled over the bed to the floor and swiftly got to work. I used our rusty flathead screw driver to take out the fresher looking screws and put them neatly on the bed, I then apprehensively lifted the floorboard half

expecting to see a pair of eyes staring back at me,

but instead I saw what looked like a small leather

briefcase inside. I pulled it out and tried to open it,

but it was locked by a number code. I tried the

obvious ones like our Birthdays and Dad and Mum's

anniversary, but nothing worked. Then I went for

Mum's date of death, and I felt a click. It worked.

"Why that date?" I thought to myself, blissfully

unaware of the horrors I was about to unearth.

I opened the briefcase and out fell a bunch of

polaroid photos, I believe there were 23 of them in

total, some face up and some face down. I saw

Mum in some lingerie in one and quickly moved my eyes away thinking this was clearly my dad's porn stash. But as I glanced away, my eyes fixed on one very familiar item.

My cat ornament was in the briefcase. Dad said he wanted to take it to work to make him feel better and so I wasn't around a potential trigger. But he put it in a secret hiding hole. I was puzzled and asked myself why he would need to lie to me. I picked it up, I frowned at it whilst looking at the bottom logo again and this time I decided to scratch off the residue to reveal the name "Barnaby Village" written on it. It meant nothing to me at the time, but I couldn't help but fixate on the name. I must've said it to myself 25 times over, I was confused as to why I couldn't stop saying it, but nothing confused me to the same the levels as when I looked at the rest of the pictures. I thought they would all be of Mum in smutty clothes and sexy poses. Which I didn't really want to see, but I was 17 and curious. So, I turned some more over.

They were the same size, but some were much dirtier than others, by 'dirtier' I mean dusty and marked up, not X-rated.
You could tell some were from a few years ago and some were much, much more recent.

In each of the Polaroids was a naked woman.

Bound. Tied. Bleeding. Maybe dead. Each of them

with a name roughly scrawled in ink along the

bottom,

"Sarah. K", "Denise. F", "Valerie. W". At least 14 of

them had readable names. I was close to vomiting

as I was surrounded by these gruesome photos

scattered across the floor. The smell that filled the

air in that moment I can still remember now. It was

earthy and somehow almost metallic, it just smelled

of something evil. There were locks of hair tied in

plaits in the case too, I didn't want to touch those at

all. I finally got to one of the last pictures, shaking

and wiping the tears from my eyes I turn over the

picture to reveal a woman, bound and beaten, her jaw snapped, and her eye gouged out. It was the same woman I saw in the mirror downstairs. "Amanda. B" it had written along the bottom.

I got a really sudden and heavy pain in my head, so I looked up and lost all concept of reality when I saw that the room was filled with of all these women, stood around me like a circle. Some were almost unrecognisable from the wounds on their faces, but I knew it was them. I then heard the bedroom door creak, so I turned to look and saw Amanda slowly walking in, one broken step at a time. She stood in front of me and made the clicking sound, her remaining eye was a milky white, her skin was dry,

cracked and a bluish grey, lacerated all over with a

large wound on the left side of her face causing her

jaw bone to practically hang off her decomposing

face.

I cried hysterically, I was terrified. My headache was

agonising as she walked up to me. Which only

amplified as I heard her bones cracking and popping

with each step until she was inches from my face. I

begged her not to hurt me and as I did that, she

lifted her hand and touched my temple and slid her

cold fingers to my jaw and squeezed gently just as

the person in the kitchen did earlier. I could feel her

broken finger nails scraping gently against my cheek as she did this. Then out of nowhere I had lost the ability to breathe. I looked at all the women in the room as I choked, they all began to vanish slowly in front of my eyes. I then looked back to Amanda, but she was gone too, as soon as the final ghostly apparition of these unfortunate souls disappeared, I could instantly breathe again.

Taking deep breaths, weeping and chilled to the bone, I collapsed to the ground and erratically shoved all the photos back in the briefcase and closed it tightly shut. As I did, I noticed another Polaroid on the ground that I must have missed. I wish I had never seen this one. It was my Mum.

Tied and bound in the same ways as these women,

but my dad was in this one, naked and sporting that

same goofy smile he always gives me. Mom was

alive in this photo, they looked to be having fun,

but she was tied in the same ways the other

women were. I immediately got hit with a harsh

reality. "Is my dad a serial killer?".

I rushed to put the briefcase back in the floor,

screwing in the screws and putting it all back just

how I found it. Weeping for the women I'd just seen

and for my own sanity after the night I'd just had.

I had so many questions that I needed answers. Just

as I covered my face to wipe the tears away, the lights came back on. The hallway lights lit the way to the living room phone, so I got up and stumbled towards the telephone. My legs felt like jelly beneath my torso. I got there and immediately thought of calling my dad, but I hesitated and wondered if I should call the police instead. Which was a thought I couldn't get right with in my mind. My head was going a million miles an hour and the pressure was giving me the most severe headache. So, I quickly snapped myself out of it, hatched an idea and decided to grab the phone book. I found and called the only other place I could think of in the haze of my terror. Barnaby Village.

I called but they were closed. I called twice more just to be sure, but it was the same result. No answer. Granted it was 4am, but I figured I needed it couldn't hurt to try them a few times.

I sat at my kitchen counter for an hour deciding what I should do. I made the decision to sweep up all the glass and wood from the hallway and tidy up all the candles, putting them back in my drawer upstairs. I walked back downstairs to put the screwdriver back in the shed when I realised it had passed 6am. So, I decided to give Barnaby Village another shot.

I dialled the number and this time it rang. My heart

sank as I heard the sound of the other end picking up and a deep, booming voice say "Barnaby Village, John Barnaby speaking, how can I help?"

I froze for a moment. "Hello?" John said all agog. I just couldn't speak and was about to hang up when I heard the man say in a soft, sorrowful tone "Amanda? Is this you? We aren't mad, sweetheart. Please come home. We miss you." I hung the phone up and jumped back from it. The girl in the photo. The girl who touched my face. "Amanda. B". I asked myself a hundred times "is her name Amanda Barnaby"?

I needed to be sure, so I ran back upstairs, equipped with the screwdriver, and got the briefcase back out in a flash. I read the name on the bottom of the ornament over and over, it wasn't a mistake. It was Barnaby Village and the photo definitely said "Amanda. B" on it. Just then, my heart skipped a beat when I heard the familiar jingle of my dad's keys once again against our front door.

The front door opened, and I heard Dad coming inside, taking his coat off. I scrabbled quickly to get the briefcase back into the floor, but to my alarm I heard him coming up the stairs before I was able to screw the screws in. I put the carpet down, moved the table back, threw the screws and the screwdriver under the bed. I hopped into his bed

and pretended to be asleep.

He came into his room and was shocked to see me

there. He then crept around putting things away.

He went over to the side of the bed where the

floorboard was, I was terrified he would notice

something out of place, but he just put something

in the drawer of his bedside table and then went

back downstairs. I quickly and quietly went to check

what he put in his drawer.

It was an unsealed envelope containing a gold

necklace with a green heart pendant and my gut

churned as I also saw another polaroid with its back

to me in there too. I turned the picture over to see

exactly what I'd feared would be printed on its face.

Another woman tied up and brutally beaten beyond

comprehension. I felt sick again but that feeling

washed away and was replaced by shock and

disgust when I saw the necklace around this

woman's neck in the photo was also the same one

in this envelope. As if it was some sort of trophy.

I delicately shut the drawer and laid down for a

moment in Dad's bed. A million and one questions

shooting back and forth in my brain like a game of

ping pong.

Then I got up, went to my room and got dressed. I

walked down the stairs and noticed nothing out of the ordinary except my knowledge of who my dad really was.

I walked into the living room and looked to the left. There he was, unpacking his bags as usual. He looked up and shot me the same goofy smile he had in the photo with my Mum. It sent a wave of sharp tingles all over my body. "Hey Kiddo. You're up early!" He said with genuine astonishment. "I hope I didn't wake you!" He said almost as if to figure out if I saw him come in to the bedroom and put the things in his drawer.

"No." I said forcing a smile. "I just went to sleep

really early last night." I stood frozen as the lie I'd

told reinforced the true memories of the previous

night, like a slideshow in my head. "You okay? You

look like you've seen a ghost, Hil." He said without

any acknowledgement of the irony surrounding

that very phrase. I looked at him, I was furious. I

wanted to kill him. But I knew that wouldn't help

anything, so I said I was just feeling rough still and

not to worry. He smiled and went back to

unpacking.

I moved to the other side of the counter, ensuring

there was a blockade between us, and asked how

his work went with an attentive look on my face. "It

was okay. Got the job done, that was the main thing." He said with a definitive change in his pitch.

As he stood up to put his toiletries on the counter, I noticed a scratch near his eyebrow, it looked nasty.

"You cut your face. How did you do that?" I said with a noticeable change in my voice too. Seeing another wound after everything I saw last night made my skin crawl.

"Oh, this?" He said pointing to his eyebrow and throwing his head back with a maniacal chuckle.

"Well, this serves me right for not wearing eye protection and using a power saw." He said boldly.

I didn't believe any word of anything he was telling

me. I knew I had to react as if I did though, so I made the right faces to indicate my sympathy and empathy for that pain. Wincing and saying it must've hurt, laughing with him when his face scrunched up as he re-enacted the moment. But when I asked him what it was that hit him in the face, his mouth uncurled quickly, his cheeks dropped suddenly as he just blankly stared at the kitchen counter for around 3 seconds, like he was thinking about what to say to me, then looked at me and bluntly said it was a "piece of wood". I said "okay" and didn't ask anything else. His tone seemed to suggest he was agitated and that never would have bothered me before. I probably would have kept on asking and laughed as he got mad at me. Probably would have been an inside joke forever. But now, now I was afraid of him. My own Father. My only living parent. A killer.

Then he asked "What happened to all the pictures?" and my stomach twisted. I didn't know what to tell him. I looked up and said "I don't know what happened, but I slipped and fell down the stairs last night. I cleaned up the mess and put the photos in the top drawer of the dresser though." He asked if I was okay and if I hurt myself to which I replied "a little on my elbow, but I'm okay. Sorry I broke so many. I'm so clumsy." He didn't seem too bothered by it. "Well, clumsiness must run in the family" he said, pointing back to his eyebrow. I feigned a laugh and looked away. Seemed being a good liar ran in the family too.

Then just as I felt like I'd dodged a bullet, I remembered something with a startling shock. The screws and screwdriver were still under his bed! He was going to put the newest Polaroid and necklace in the briefcase with the rest of his morbid collection and see they were unscrewed and know that I know!

I needed to get him out of the house so I could screw them back in. So, he would never know that I knew. I told him quickly, almost without thinking that he needed to go to the shop. He looked at me with a furled brow, puzzled and asked "why?". I searched for a reason in my mind and the only one I could think of was "because I just got my period, and I don't have any pads". His eyebrows raised. He got up, walked around the counter and kissed my head. I flinched when he touched my shoulder. "Back in a sec" he said with a wink and walked out holding his keys.

I just ran for it. I ran up the stairs so fast I gave myself carpet burn on my toes. I dropped on my front at the side of his bed and immediately grabbed the screws and screwdriver. Shakily

screwing them in and uttering words of

encouragement under my breath as if it would help

convince the screws to go in first try. But I was

going so quickly that they fell over a few times

before I actually got them in properly. After I did, I

immediately ran down the stairs and out the

backdoor to put the screwdriver back in the shed,

when walking to come back inside, I saw the ghostly

entities of these poor women in the windows of

every room. Watching me. Staring at me, almost

through me. I knew what I had to do.

I walked inside and could hear the rattling on the

floorboards and the clicking of Amanda's tongue

sending freezing shivers down my spine. I knew I

needed to call the police, so I picked up the phone

and dialled the number.

It rang twice before the operator answered, I said I

needed the police and waited for the transfer. But

as I was waiting, I heard Dad's keys in the door, so I

quickly hung up.

He walked in the living room and bounded straight

over to me, handed me some pads along with a

sympathetic smile. I shakily said "thank you" and

went upstairs to my room.

I stayed there for hours and hours. I tried sleeping

again but I couldn't. I couldn't get the images of

those women out of my head. I think I reread

probably about 20 issues of Volkat Warrior Queen

to take my mind off it. I kept hearing him moving

stuff around in his room, until he went downstairs.

It was about an hour that went by before I heard

Dad call me downstairs for dinner. I wasn't hungry

at all, my appetite was gone. But I mustered up the

energy to walk down the stairs. I could smell the

aroma of my dad's famous homemade curry getting

stronger with each step I took.

I walked in and sat at the kitchen counter where

Dad had left me a bowl full of his curry. He was sat

on the other side of the counter eating his portion

like a ravenous beast. He looked at me and told me

how proud he was of me. How much I've been

forced to grow up this year and how well I've

handled the loss of my Mum. He told me that he

loved me and that he had something to tell me.

"I've got some good news and some bad news" he

said. I asked what the bad news was, and he told

me "Sadly, I set your cat ornament on my desk at

the build site for luck and it got knocked off and

smashed into a million pieces. I'm so sorry.". My

face must've looked horrified, because I knew he

was lying, but this was different because I knew it

was upstairs under the floor. Dad saw my face and

must have misconstrued it as sadness at the loss of the ornament because he tilted his head with a pout and said "I know, honey. I'm so sorry. But the good news is I did buy you a little gift to show you how sorry I am." He then handed me a small box that gave off a quiet rattle as he slid it across the counter. I opened the box to find a necklace. Not just any necklace though. A gold necklace with a green heart pendant. The very same necklace that was in the drawer upstairs. The very same necklace that was around the bruised neck of the woman in the new polaroid.

Suddenly I felt myself fall away into a labyrinthine

trance of memories, all the times Dad went to work

far away, all the times he would come back early &

have these cuts on his face and hands but say it was

from work, every joke, every laugh, every smile,

everything I ever knew about this man had been a

lie. My trance ended as I stared at the necklace and

whispered through tears of rage and despair

"where did you get this from"?

"From another second hand shop, I know you like

vintage stuff" he said very quickly. I thought he

must have rehearsed that one in the van a few

times.

I looked up at him and he said "oh sweetie, no need

to cry, it didn't cost a lot or anything. I just saw it

and thought of you."

He took a huge mouthful of curry as he said it.

He noticed that I'd not touched my food yet and

said "Well dig in. It's got ginger in it. Your

favourite!", it was a favourite of mine, but I wasn't

hungry. I had millions of questions, and I was

fighting every single voice in my head telling me to

just blurt them out. But I held my tongue.

I told him I was still feeling under the weather and

asked if he would mind if I kept my dinner in the

oven for later, he said he didn't mind, but couldn't

guarantee he wouldn't eat it before then and

laughed. I gave an uncomfortable grin as I slowly
walked out.

I went to my room and just cried and cried. I
couldn't believe this was my reality. I needed to
wait for him to fall asleep so I could call the police.
But then I had a terrifying thought, what if he
noticed his grisly stash was all out of order? What if
he got rid of it all and then when I called the police,
they'd have come and found nothing, he would've
gotten off the hook and then I'd have been left
there with him knowing that I knew? What was that
level of hell going to look like?

I needed to be sure, and, in that moment, I knew I

needed to scrap the whole idea of calling the police.

I just needed to get the whole collection and run to

the police station with it all. So, I sat in my room

and prepared.

After a while, I heard my dad's lumbering feet on

the stairs. Stomp, stomp, stomping his way up. I got

in bed and turned my back to the door to pretend I

was sleeping. I heard a gentle knock on my door

before hearing it slightly open. "Good night, honey"

I heard Dad whisper, I'd wondered if he knew I was

awake, but I stayed silent anyway and he just shut

the door.

I waited for what felt like an eternity for him to

sleep, but no matter how hard I fought it off, the lack of sleep caught up to me and I dozed off. When I woke up, the moon was full and it was so dark but for the moon shining into my room, almost identical to the night prior. Only this time I saw the ghostly faces of 17 women in my room, in the shadows, staring at me without blinking. I was petrified but it was a little easier to process this time. I noticed quickly that I actually recognised them all. Their abuse images were burned into my brain so heavily that I could even name most of them.

Except Amanda, she wasn't there.

When I turned to get out of bed, I was met by the

sunken face of the brutally beaten Amanda just inches from my nose. Staring her single milky white eye into my two tear-filled eyes, she climbed onto my bed very slowly whilst making the clicking sound very fast this time. I moved backwards and stepped off the bed, but as soon as my foot touched my floor, I got another excruciating headache, and someone had grabbed my ankle from under the bed, so I fell. Just as I hit the floor, Amanda collapsed off the bed and crawled on top of me. I could smell the putrid scent of her rotten rattling breath, see the decomposing wounds on her body and even hear her jaw bones clunking together as she tilted her head. I wanted to scream, but I couldn't. One again all the air in my lungs was

trapped, as if I was being strangled when in the

presence of Amanda. I just about got out a squeak

of asking her not to hurt me and she immediately

dissipated into a cloud of vapour.

I took some deep breaths as I was anxiously looking

around my room, darting my eyes front to back

looking for any sign of the women. I scrabbled to

my feet. The coast was clear. I opened my door a

crack and could hear Dad snoring next door. So, I

tiptoed down the stairs and into the kitchen,

making sure I didn't make a single sound. I had

memorised every floorboard in that house when I

used to sneak out at night to see my friends, which ones made a sound and which ones were loud enough to wake up the neighbourhood. So, I was confident in navigating that wooden minefield. Once downstairs, I got my boots on and went outside to the shed to retrieve the screwdriver.

As I approached the shed in the blistering winter winds, I looked up at the windows expecting to see the spectral forms of the women again, but they weren't there. I was relieved, because they weren't all that pleasant to look at. So, I quickly unlocked the padlock on the bolted up shed door and got the screwdriver. I locked the door back up in a hurry and turned around to see that I was surrounded by the phantom forms of the naked, lacerated, broken women one more. The sight of them frightened me so much that I fell back with a sharp jolt which caused me to drop the screwdriver on the frosty grass. I shakily bent down quickly to pick it up and when I came back up, they were all gone again. Somehow, I didn't feel scared though. Now I felt determined.

I went inside and quietly slid the door shut. Listening out for Dad's footsteps upstairs. But all I heard when I truly listened were his loud snores rattling through the house.

I walked through the kitchen and living room feeling like, out of the corners of my eyes, I was seeing the women in the dark corners of every room. I got to the stairs, ascended them quieter than ever before, even quieter than when I used to sneak out to see my friends in the middle of the night. I reached the top and saw Dad's door was shut. I snuck up to the door and gently rotated the doorknob until the door made an ear piercing shunting sound. I stayed dead still as I was so sure it woke him, but after staying still for a few moments, I heard the snores again.

I slowly opened the door and peered in. Dad was

sleeping on his front on the side closest to the door, which was the other side of floorboard I needed to unscrew. "Perfect" I thought to myself. I crept in on my hands and knees, glancing up at Dad with every movement I made. He stayed sleeping and snoring away.

I got to the other side of the bed and managed to lift the bedside table up and place it down making almost no noise at all. All that was left to do was peel back the carpet, unscrew the screws, grab the briefcase and get out of the house.

I quickly yanked the carpet back and whipped out the screwdriver from my hoodie pocket. I unscrewed all 4 screws, reached inside the hole and

grabbed the briefcase. I was both relieved and

mortified to know it was still there.

I pulled it out quietly, making sure to keep it level

and not knock anything around that was inside.

When I got it out, I unlocked it to check it was all

still there. It was.

But then I noticed the new Polaroid had a name

scribbled on it. "Ginger".

I had another involuntary trance-like surge of

memories. Remembering the meals Dad would

make after his trips. How the meat was usually

wrapped in a piece of paper when he got it out,

how he seasoned it the same way almost every

time, then I remember what he said at the dinner

table this evening. "It's got Ginger in it." Before I

could even begin to fathom what he might have

meant I felt a slight lick of warm air on my cheek, I

turned to look at what it was and saw my dad,

leaning off his bed and staring at me in a way I'd

never seen before. Like his face wasn't *his* face

anymore.

I fought back the tears as I sat back terrified. "That's

my stuff, Hil. You don't have any right to look at

that." He said through clenched teeth. "You've been

a very, very bad girl, Hillary." he continued.

I still had a firm hold of the briefcase, the front door

was only out his door, down the stairs and straight in front of me. I thought I could make a run for it.

As I sprung up to my feet, Dad got out of bed on the side closest to me. I ran past him towards the door, and he jumped over the bed and slammed the door shut, standing in front of it with a smirk on his face. "Listen, I love you and I want to talk to you about this." He said with a soft tone masking his snarl. "You killed these women, Dad" I said, barely making any sense through the shaking in my throat. "You're a murderer.".

He turned his head and closed his eyes as if the word "murderer" genuinely pained him to hear.

"No, I'm not. Don't you ever say that to me again. You don't want to end up like your mother" He snapped. Immediately after that he made an expression of someone who had said too much. My eyes filled with tears and my jaw dropped with a shudder. "Did you.." I began to say but he cut me off by saying "just give me the briefcase and we can talk about it all, I promise." He extended his hand, and I shook my head whilst still tightly clutching the briefcase.

He told me to stop being stupid and to give him the case, but I continued to shake my head as the tears streamed down my face, my eyes stinging from the lack of sleep and constant tears being shed. "I am going to the police, Dad. This ends now." I said through heavy breaths and strained vocals. "Oh, Hillary. Why did you have to go and say something like that?" He said with a tilted head and look of concern.

We stood in silence for a minute or so, I could hear the rain starting to fall and the cars outside driving past the houses in my street, totally oblivious to what was happening behind the closed doors of this one. I leapt to the other side of the bed, and he sharply chased me around it. I was terrified but the adrenaline of the moment kept me going. I tried to jump over the bed, but couldn't quite make it and

landed half way across, tripping over his thick duvet

and crawling for the door when I felt his massive

hand grab my ankle and squeeze really hard.

"Hillary stop acting like this" he said vociferously as

I reached for the door, but his strength was too

much. He was dragging me back toward him. I

turned to look at him and he gave me that goofy

smile and said "you've never looked more like your

Mum", he yanked me back and I hit my hip on his

bedframe, I then used my other free foot to kick

him in the face. Which felt unnatural, kicking my

own Father in the face. Then again, what about any

of this felt natural?

As I kicked him, he grabbed my right leg and crossed it under my left knee and bent my left leg downward whilst placing his arm through the gap in my thighs. I was stuck and he was lifting me upside down by my crossed legs. The pain was inexplicable, but as I let out a scream the screwdriver fell from my hoodie pocket and hit the ground right by my face.

I grabbed it and didn't think twice. I stabbed his hand so hard that the head of the screwdriver went through his whole hand and into my own leg.

Thankfully the way he recoiled and pulled his hand

back made him let me go and pull the screw driver out of my leg simultaneously. I was finally able to open his bedroom door.

I ran with a limp towards the stairs, but Dad leapt from the room and grabbed me so we both came tumbling down the stairs. I felt a sharp pain in my right forearm, but I ignored it and just got up to run to the door as Dad laid their motionless, I tried to open the door, but it was locked. The keys were hanging by the top of the door, so I reached up to get them with my right hand and almost fainted when I saw the bone of my arm sticking out of the skin. It was in that moment when I heard Dad groaning and getting up.

I knew I needed to get out of there. So, I put the briefcase handle in my mouth and used my left hand to get the keys and unlock the door. I just left the keys in the door and ran for it, faster than I've ever ran before. Even with the limp and blood gushing from my leg.

As I was running, I heard Dad call my name, but I didn't even look back. I just ran. Once I got some distance, I took a shortcut through the old school, no one was there because it was due to be torn down the following month, so I was thinking it would save me time, but just as I approached the end of the entrance, Dad's van pulled up with a squeal of the tyres.

As soon as I heard the pop of his car door opening, I ran inside the school grounds and saw that there were lots of skips filled with broken desks and old flooring tiles from the school, so I hid behind one. I heard the school gate screech as it's rusty hinges swung open, the sound was soon followed by Dad's sinister shadow illuminated by his headlights. He was practically skipping as he entered the school grounds, whistling to himself.
The fact he was so calm made me so unsure of myself in that moment.

Like he knew something I didn't, and he already had

me right where he wanted me.

"Hillary. I know you're here. I don't want to play

hide and seek. Come out and talk. Please?" He said

very softly, as if he could sense I was nearby.

"Honey, I don't want to fight." He said with a jovial

chuckle, trying to lure me out with niceties. I didn't

dare respond.

"Hillary!" he shouted vehemently, and it echoed in

the empty construction site of a schoolyard. "I'm

not asking." He said through tightly clenched teeth.

He stopped for a moment, took a deep breath and

serenely said "let's just calm down, go home and

talk this out."

I could see him through a small crack in the side of
the skip I was behind, he looked like he saw
something and took off running into the dark school
field next to us. So, I decided to take the
opportunity and run like the wind through the site. I
hopped over gates and maneuvered around every
cement truck and white van parked on the grounds.
I got to the end, where I was due to exit, but every
way out was blocked by large fences with barbed
wire lining the tops. I decided that wasn't going to
be enough to stop me, so I decided to again hold
the briefcase handle in my mouth, grab the fence

with my one good hand and start climbing. I got about halfway up before an icy cold shiver went up my spine. "That's a hell of a climb, Hil. Careful you don't fall and break your neck." I heard it from directly below me, I turned and looked down, there he was. Dad had found me.

He grabbed my jeans with his still blood soaked and bleeding hand and grabbed the back of my hoodie with his other hand and just yanked me off the fence, slamming me into the ground on my back. I felt all the air leave my lungs and the back of my head hit on the concrete, making it bleed from the crown. "Please" I said rolling over to my front. A sudden deep pain came coursing through my abdomen as he kicked me in the ribs. He started mocking the way I was talking and laughing at my pleas. "Please, Dad. Stop!" I begged him. "Daddy. It's me, it's Hil! Stop it!" I said through my shuddering and winded voice box. "No!" He bellowed with a growl. "You could have been. But you just had to go snooping, didn't you? Making your little assumptions about your old man. You're all the same." He spat with another sharp punt to my already bruising ribcage. "No. I know exactly who you are." He uttered whilst standing on my broken wrist, grinning with gloating glee as I tried to scream out in agony. "You're my 20th." it was then when he started punching me in the face

repeatedly, I could taste the blood in my mouth as I

spat out 2 of my back teeth. He laughed at me as I

cried in pain, both physical and emotional. He gave

my ribs a few more kicks and then knelt one knee

on my back as I tried to crawl away.

I was trying to scream for help, but my voice wasn't

working. His knee was cutting off my air. It was then

I felt the scratchy fibres of the rope around my neck

and the tension in my spine as he was pulling back

on the rope with force. After about 20 seconds, I

heard a ringing in my ears, my periphery went

blurry, and I was losing the will to fight on. He was

killing me.

At that moment, I truly believed I was done for. But then a sudden flash of white came across my vision, and I saw, in blazing light, all of the women surrounding us in a circle and my dad jumped off of me in an instant.

Scrabbling for all the oxygen I could get in my constricted windpipe I managed to get to a tree stump and pull myself up. Dad was in the circle surrounded by the ghosts of his past fatalities and was screaming "No! You're not here. None of you are real!" Crawling backwards towards the fences. It was then, I felt that piercing pain in my temple again and my jaw clenched shut as the ringing in my

ear became unbearable. The pain reached a peak

and then quickly faded as I heard a soft voice call

my name, a familiar voice that caused the hairs on

my neck to stand up. I turned and saw her.

Blindingly beautiful as ever but looked so sad. It

was my mother. I wanted to cry but didn't have the

time nor would the sounds come out of my mouth.

Mum put her finger to her lips and pointed to the

bushes on the corner and said "Run, baby.".

I quickly picked up the briefcase and ran as fast as I

could to get to the bushes whilst Dad was writhing

around on the floor being tormented by the soul

splitting stares of his returning victims. I'd found an

opening.

I climbed through thorns and nettles, spider webs and I'm pretty sure a few broken bottles and used syringes too. But I made it to the other side. Around the corner from the Police Station.

I ran, then limped as my legs got heavy. Then crawled to the Station door as my body finally gave way under all abuse it had taken. I stood and tapped on the door, which was locked at night, but I was immediately buzzed in by the Officer on the reception desk. Once I got in, the Officer who let me in, Officer Shepherd, just looked at me, gasped and said "What's happened, love?" and I just lost it.

All the tears I'd cried, I cried again, all the pain was

amplified, and the heartbreak was unspeakable.

She came running over, wrapped her arm around

me and took me to a room and I told her what I'd

found. I showed her the briefcase and all of its

contents. I also explained the lock code number and

that I didn't know what happened to my Mum

anymore.

Within 20 minutes the police were out looking for

Dad. I stayed in the Station for the rest of the night

with Officer Shepherd, talking about everything. It

had been hours but was around 8am when I heard

them come in the Station doors, booking a person

into a holding cell. They said a name. It was Dad's. I walked out and saw him standing with 3 Policemen. Hands behind his back in handcuffs. Looking very sorry for himself. He looked at me and it felt like my heart stopped and time stood still. But all I could do was give him a goofy smile and a middle finger before walking back in the room I was in and closing the door behind me.

I cried for about a week after that night.

That was almost 26 years ago now and this is the first time I'm writing it down. I've only ever told 3 people about this before. Because I don't like to talk about it. Not even when doing my seminars or touring the country doing shows. When the Court asked me how I'd found the briefcase, I realised very fast that I needed to lie. So, I said I saw him knelt down by his bed one day with a screwdriver and wondered why. So, being a nosy teenager, I just went to find out when he was out of the house for the night. Because I wasn't stupid, I knew if I'd have said "oh, the ghosts made me look there." I'd have looked like an immature, crazy child and his lawyers would have torn me apart on the stand. They would never have taken me seriously. Which was the last thing the world needed when a serial killer's freedom was at stake.

Dad though, he went down that road. Telling

everyone about the ghosts that attacked him,

admitting to the murders whilst doing so. Also

admitting to not only killing these poor women, but

also confessing that he'd tortured and eaten them

too, or parts of them anyway.

He also admitted to feeding both my Mum and I the

meat. Which is beyond repulsive and still gives me a

knot in my tummy even now. He got life with no

possibility of parole, he plead insanity and got it.

Being placed in Bausinden Hospital for the

Criminally Insane.

The press dubbed him the "Clifton Cannibal", like

he needed a moniker to boast about. He loves the notoriety even now. During the rest of the 1990s and most of the 2000s he had promised to lead investigators to the various burial sites of his 19 victims, the investigators would take him all over the country, give him lunch, buy his drinks and cigarettes all day, then when they would get to the supposed grave sites, he would decide he wasn't going to give them the information after all. He was grilled and interrogated for months when he got arrested, but hardly gave any real information as to what he did to the bodies of these women after he'd murdered them. He is still revealing tiny titbits of information as to where he buried the bodies or how he disposed of them 21 years later, but no one takes him seriously anymore.

Dad loves the attention of it all. He's written to me approximately five thousand times over the years, but I've never once responded. He's dead to me and has been for 26 years. He most recently had the newspapers write a story that he'd only divulge the information of where the bodies are to me. Which I know is just a last ditch effort to get my attention, but I can't help but wonder if he's finally telling the truth.

I never saw my Mum again. Or any of those unfortunate souls for that matter, except for

Amanda, but I sometimes still feel them around me.

Amanda isn't the same broken, beaten woman I

first saw anymore either. Seems she was able to

move on after Dad was brought to justice. She is so

beautiful. I see her all the time. She assists me

whenever I am stuck or need guidance. I'm very

lucky to have her presence in my life.

After Dad was in police custody, our neighbour took

me in for a while but being around the house

wasn't doing my head any good. I was having

nightmares and couldn't stop myself from thinking

about it all every minute of every day. After 3

months or so, I called Amanda's parents back and

spoke to them. John and Christie Barnaby. I thought

they would hate me for what my dad had done, but

it was the opposite. It became a regular thing that I

would call them, then that evolved into going to

their house for cups of tea. Then soon going over

for dinners and sleepovers and eventually they

invited me to live with them. At first, I thought it

was out of pity, but they treated me like I was their

own daughter, moved me in, fed me, clothed me,

paid for me to go to university & they even helped

me start up my business. They were the only ones I

ever talked about seeing Amanda and how she'd

helped me and showed me the way to the truth.

They knew I wasn't lying because I could tell them

very specific things about her childhood that no one else knew and I only knew them because Amanda was telling me as I was telling them. They would cry tears of joy most days knowing their little girl was still with them.

So, I guess I could do the whole *"Doctor's Notes"* thing here but I'm going to do this last part differently because this really isn't just the story of how my world came crashing down and finding out that my dad was a serial killer. This is the story of how I discovered my incredible gift, my first experience and what it led to. Seeing the closure these families got when they heard about their loved ones being confirmed as one of Dad's victims was bittersweet to say the least, but I wanted to do more of it. It seemed to truly unlock the floodgates of grief and allow it to wash over them. They finally had an answer, even if it wasn't one they wanted to hear, at least they finally knew. I wanted to help bring people to justice and bring families of missing loved ones some peace. So that's what I do now, I work as a Psychic Detective, among other things like touring, writing, putting on webinars and speaking at conventions. I've even been on TV a couple of times helping a team of Paranormal Investigators. So, my life has turned out pretty good so far, all things considered.

For a long time I suffered with nightmares, I was anxious all the time, I'd be startled by the faintest of noises. I was fearful of my own shadow. But one day I figured out that you can't look forward to anything if you're always looking over your shoulder. I learned a lot from the whole ordeal. More than anyone will ever know. But most importantly I learned a very important lesson. Assume nothing. Just because you know a person doesn't mean you *know* the real person behind the mask they wear. That's not to say everyone is wearing one, but it's good to be wary. Protect yourself. I also learned that a person could go through Hell and come out of it stronger with the

right support and determination.

Thank you for reading. This is my story.

- Dr Hillary Johnstone.

Printed in Great Britain
by Amazon

16108249R00257